THE
PICKLED APOCALYPSE
OF PANCAKE ISLAND

ALSO BY CAMERON PIERCE

Shark Hunting in Paradise Garden
Ass Goblins of Auschwitz
Lost in Cat Brain Land

THE PICKLED APOCALYPSE OF PANCAKE ISLAND

A Tragedy for People Who Eat Food

CAMERON PIERCE

Eraserhead Press
Portland, OR

ERASERHEAD PRESS
205 NE BRYANT
PORTLAND, OR 97211

WWW.ERASERHEADPRESS.COM

ISBN: 1-936383-08-X

Copyright © 2010 by Cameron Pierce

Cover art copyright © 2010 by Alan M. Clark
http://www.alanmclark.com/

Interior art copyright © 2010 by Sam Pink

All rights reserved. No part of this book may be reproduced or transmitted in any form or by any means, electronic or mechanical, including photocopying, recording, or by any information storage and retrieval system, without the written consent of the publisher, except where permitted by law.

Printed in the USA.

For Kirsten. Let's eat Fod forever.

An eternal thanks goes out to the following people. They will go down as legends, for they made the pickled apocalypse happen:

Rhys Alton, Piers Anthony, Forrest Armstrong, Jeff Burk, Joshua Byrnes, Alan M. Clark, Danielle Clark, Edmund Colell, Justin Coons, Ray Dittmeier, Anthony Fischer, Corrinne Garrison, Mykle Hansen, Chrissy Horchheimer, Jeremy Robert Johnson, Vince Kramer, Michael Livsey, Nicola McClements, Carlton Mellick III, Angela Molinar, Rose O'Keefe, Kelly Pierce, Sam Pink, Andersen Prunty, Sam Reeve, Rachel Roeske, Michael Rose, Michael Sauers, Kevin Shamel, Jay Sigler, Shane Sinsapaugh, Bruce Taylor, and Richard Tingley

"I wish I had been hungry for a hamburger instead of bullets."
    - Richard Brautigan, *So the Wind Won't Blow it All Away*

"A vulturous boredom pinned me in this tree.
 If he were I, he would do what I did."
    - Sylvia Plath, *The Hanging Man*

"And we could be happy
 And we could be happy
 And we could be happy
 And we could be happy"
    - Daniel Johnston, *The Monster Inside Of Me*

PART ONE

THE MOST BEAUTIFUL PANCAKE IN THE UNIVERSE

FANNY WINTER FOD

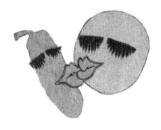

Fanny W. Fod had peanut butter lips, blueberry eyes, chocolate chip dimples, and hair softer than cinnamon. She lactated the most delicious maple beer in the universe, and she bottled and distributed her beer all around Pancake Island. The pancakes loved her beer. They savored it to the last drop. They would wave and call out, "Thank you, Fanny Fod!" They would cheer, "Hooray, we're so happy. Let's be happy forever. Let's hold a parade for happiness." And so the pancakes savored the beer of Fanny Fod and commenced their daily Ultra Yummy Happiness Parade.

What they did not know was that Fanny Fod, the most beautiful pancake in the universe, felt sick inside her soul.

It was nighttime on Pancake Island. The pancake sun snoozed in his bed of stars. His mustache glowed like a furry nightlight.

Fanny Fod lay on her back on the roof of her green zucchini castle. Every pancake lived in a castle, but Fanny's was the only castle built out of zucchinis. However, this caused no jealousy among the pancakes. The others were happy with their potato castles. Potato castles were special too. As potato castles got older, they grew spuds that turned into other potato castles. After many years of living in potato castles, it was as if all the pancakes lived in one giant interconnected spud kingdom, except for Fanny Fod, because she chose to live alone.

Fanny Fod, the most beautiful pancake on the island, lay on her back on the roof of her zucchini castle and stared out at the stars. She knew there were a lot of sad creatures in the universe. She wished she could help them. Maybe she could bottle her syrup and launch the bottles into outer space. Maybe somewhere out there a sad creature longed for monogamy just like she did.

Fanny Fod longed for a sad creature to love and make happy. She had been romantically involved with many pancakes, but the love between two happy creatures was just too sweet.

Happiness was all she'd ever felt. She wondered what sadness was like. There must be something else, she thought. There must be something besides happiness. She knew something strange was happening for her to think this because everybody loved happiness and she loved happiness too. She was always happy, but some nights she wished she wasn't. She pondered whether the Cuddlywumpus locked in the dungeon of her zucchini castle was affecting her in some way. Or maybe these strange thoughts and feelings—nostalgia and longing for abstract or nonexistent things—thoughts and feelings that were not exactly happy but resulted in happiness because she desired them—maybe all pancakes experienced these things, just nobody talked about them.

Maybe it was really the Cuddlywumpus. She was afraid of the Cuddlywumpus. She was afraid some other pancake would find out about the Cuddlywumpus. The Cuddlywumpus was her big secret. She wondered if all pancakes had a big secret that they kept to themselves.

Fanny Fod closed her eyes so she didn't have to look at the stars dancing around the sun's mustache anymore. She stood up with her eyes closed and groped her way to the zucchini spires. She rested her spongy elbows on the ledge. She leaned out, her eyes still closed. She wondered what would happen if she fell. If she jumped. It's all the same to fall or jump, she thought. Given the choice, though, between falling or jumping, I would jump every time. Too bad I am happy. If I were to jump, or even fall by accident, I would rise, because that's all I'm capable of. Happy things just rise. I could splatter to pieces amidst the pancake flowers in the front yard, and I would still be rising. Even when they are hitting bottom, happy things continue to rise. When you are happy, everything gets better all the time. Are things getting better for me, she wondered, or is this more of the same life?

PART TWO

THE PICKLED DIARIES

ROCKET SHIP FOR SAD DAY PARTY

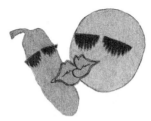

Hello, my name is Gaston Glew.

I felt suicidal this morning, so I stumbled outside and stood in the brinestorm. My sixteenth Sad Day party was scheduled for today. That's why I was suicidal, and also because I was born a pickle. All pickles kill themselves sooner or later. Anyway, back to my Sad Day party.

Mother tried baking me a cake but she slit her wrists instead. Father got so worried, he had an epileptic fit. I took my single present to my room. Alone, I unclasped the rusted latch of the mildewed wooden box. There was nothing inside. My parents had been so depressed, they forgot to buy me the customary sixteenth Sad Day present: a shotgun.

I dropped the box underfoot and stomped it into splintered scraps. I decided I would leave this place forever. I had reached this decision a long time ago. I hated Pickled Planet. I hated my fellow pickles. I hated brine. Every pickle received a shotgun on their sixteenth Sad Day, but not me. I guess I'm not your ordinary pickle. I don't worship my sadness.

We were in the living room. Father and Mother lay side by side on the floor. They had blank expressions on their faces. Mother's wrists bled.

"Father?"

"Yes son?"

"Will you buy me Captain Pickle brand rocket thrusters? My rocket ship needs them. It's my Sad Day."

"Isn't the Nothing enough? Your Mother strained herself wrapping it this morning."

"I deserve more for my sixteenth Sad Day, don't I?"

"No, you don't," Father said. "Go on now. Go away. Waste your own time. Build that stupid ship of yours. I don't care."

Father rolled onto his side and yelled at Mother. He called her pathetic. He called their marriage a disappointment. He called me a walking abortion. He called her pitiful. I left them lying on the floor and walked into the kitchen.

I opened the back door and shut it quietly behind me. I shivered.

The fallen, mold-flowering cacti twitching in the muddy yard reached their arms to the algae nooses hanging from the sky. Brinestorms made the cacti sick. I thought how lucky they were to be just physically ill.

The brinestorm cast a yellow glow on everything.

I bent over and dug beneath a cactus. I lifted a handful of garlic spiders out of the mud. I needed them to complete my rocket ship. Garlic spiders relied on cacti for nourishment, so they were easy to find. I pocketed spiders until my rubber trousers bulged.

I returned to our green, dome-shaped house and went straight to my room. I took my rocket ship out of the closet and set it on the floor, parallel to my bed.

My rocket ship was almost ready for takeoff. I would finish it today. I would launch into space at nightfall. I would discover happiness and never feel sad again.

I removed the tool kit from beneath the bed and set it between the bed and the rocket ship. The hollow craft was carved from the corpse of a pickle who'd been twice as large as me, allowing room for brine chowder, for when I got hungry on the journey.

I crawled into the cockpit and nailed a garlic spider to the control panel. Its pale guts splattered across my hands.

I nailed more garlic spiders to the panel. Their white, cloven abdomens formed perfect, tender buttons. They squeaked and pleaded as the nails pierced their squishy skulls. I pretended they were me, or I was them, but even fantasies of death failed to make me happy. That was the Eternal Plight of the Pickle. We were always sad.

I couldn't take it anymore. I had to leave it all behind.

The Eternal Plight of the Pickle started a few hundred years ago, when the climate of Pickled Planet changed drastically. Our ancestors, who called themselves cucumbers and named this world Cucumber Planet, left behind a lot of books and pictures about the transformations that swept over the world. There used to be all kinds of joyful weather, like Happy Hurricanes and Smiling Tsunamis. The weather spread so much happiness that all the cucumbers danced and played and laughed every day of their lives. They were healthy creatures. They were glad. Even death was a fabulous affair in those times.

A few cucumbers had the foresight to stockpile happy feelings in bottles and cans, but when the joyful weather turned sad and briny, their reserves quickly diminished. The cucumbers evolved with the evolving planet. In the span of a few years, Absolute Happiness became Absolute Sadness. Cucumbers became pickles.

We called our pickled plight eternal because misery was everything to our race. Nobody felt good about anything, not even for a second. If not for the books and pictures left behind by our ancestors, no pickle would know sadness's polarity had ever existed.

There was a little bit of hope in knowing that somewhere in the universe, a little happiness might remain. That smudge of hope soured our pickled hearts a little more. That hope made the sadness just a little bit too much to take. I could not continue worshipping my sadness like the rest of these pickles. I had to leave the sadness behind, no matter what awaited me.

Unchain yourself from this briny fate, oh pickled prisoner! was written in cactus blood on the side of my rocket ship.

Unchain yourself from this briny fate, oh pickled prisoner! was the motto of Captain Pickle, the superhero we loved to hate. When we watched his television show, we screamed obscenities at the screen. We clawed at our faces and rolled on the ground. Our loathing for Captain Pickle made us insane. Secretly, I admired Captain Pickle. I'd scrawled his motto on the side of my rocket ship because even if we never transcended the sorrows of our brine, even if the laws of the universe preordained us to fail, failing was no excuse to avoid trying.

I had to blast off into space and search for happiness, no matter how small or inconsequential. No matter how gracelessly I failed.

Even if I discovered happiness, would I recognize it?

All I knew of happiness had been learned from the words and pictures forged by dead vegetables. I often lay awake at night and wondered if happiness was a lie.

I killed garlic spiders until I ran out of nails. I felt so weak and tired; I could not hold the hammer. I was ashamed of my ship. It disappointed me. I disappointed myself. I would never finish it. I would never fly away from

Pickled Planet. I'd prostrated myself for a dream, and all for nothing. I stroked the crushed abdomen of a garlic spider and wished that I'd been born a cactus. I whispered quietly to the twitching dead thing.

I understood none of the words that I whispered.

Depression killed my mind.

I crawled inside my spaceship and shivered in the cockpit. Besides the pickled framework, the whole ship was built of garlic spiders, hammer nails, and the feces of my family. The feces was the hardest material to acquire because we were all too constipated to move our bowels most weeks. My ship was rotten, decay upon decay. I had to finish it before the whole thing fell apart. I got out of the ship and read Captain Pickle's motto. I popped a bubble of green paint in the slogan's crooked exclamation point. I felt a little bit better.

I needed two rocket boosters to lift me from this crazy planet forever. What could I use for rocket boosters?

I looked around my room, at the bare walls and molded carpet. I owned next to nothing. The cacti in the yard could work, but I did not think cacti deserved to be happy. They were too stupid.

I left my room and shuffled down the hall. I kept my eyes on my feet. I jostled my shriveled brain for ideas. If only Father was kinder.

I opened the back door, but a *swaying* in the kitchen grabbed my attention. I looked up at a tall, slender, pickle-shaped object, precisely what I needed for a rocket booster. I thought it was a ghost. Pickled ghosts were sly, so I hurried into the kitchen before it had a chance to sneak away.

I felt like shouting, "I've got you now."

I did not shout.

I leaped from the hallway to the kitchen in a single bound. I clutched the air. The ghost was not what I'd perceived. The ghost was Father, hanging from the kitchen rafters.

"Father?"

I hopped up and down to grab the rope coiled and knotted around his neck. I thought maybe he'd decided to play a Sad Day joke on me by falsely hanging himself. Since the day Mother birthed me, I had perceived in Father a melancholy that transcended suicide.

I dug my nails into his sides. His flesh came off in strips, gumming up beneath my fingernails.

I was angry. I felt like the victim of an unspeakable crime. Today was *my* Sad Day. Father had to go and cast a shadow over everything. What kind of Father died on the anniversary of his son's tragic birth? I did not pause to mourn. I had to get Father down from the rafters. His corpse would make a wonderful rocket booster.

The noose around his midsection unraveled and he crashed down on top of me. I pushed him off. He weighed less than a can of pickled chowder. Nearly four feet long, he stretched longer by a foot than me, but I weighed more like ten cans of pickled chowder. Father had been a little anorexic. Mother and I were always on his case.

Father's flesh darkened from green to black as I carried him to my room.

There were two slots on each side of the rocket. I loaded Father into one of them. I slid him in so that his head faced outward. If I discovered any happiness in outer space, the happiness might bless his carcass with a peaceful rot. Being dead was supposed to hurt a lot more than dying itself. Seeing him loaded into Booster Slot #1, I retracted my feelings from a few minutes earlier, when I found him hanging. His suicide wasn't lousy. It was fortuitous.

I felt bad for Mother. She was unfit to live alone. I walked down the hall to the living room. She was asleep on the living room floor. I knelt beside her. I shook her lightly and said, "Father died."

No reply.

"Mother?"

I shook her again.

I saw the cuts down her arms and realized she'd done it this time. My Sad Day had turned into a family death party. I wondered if they'd planned this all along and shed three tears, one and a half tears for each parent.

I slung Mother over my back and returned to the rocket ship. I loaded her into Booster Slot #2. I loaded several cases of brine chowder into the storage compartment, put on my yellow spacesuit, and dragged my rocket ship from my bedroom into the backyard. The brinestorm had subsided. Conditions were ideal for takeoff.

I crawled into the cockpit and buckled myself in. I had to take off as soon as possible.

I pressed a few white spider buttons and the rocket boosters ignited. Mother and Father would burn to ash soon, hopefully before they woke up out of death.

"You better watch out, happiness, 'cause I'm coming for you," I said.

I was escaping the Eternal Plight of the Pickle forever.

From way up high, Pickled Planet seemed like a place you might want to visit. The pea soup tinge appeared rich and fertile even though the soil nurtured nothing livelier than cacti since the Cucumber Days ended.

My breaths came easier. I took in more air and held it in for longer. I felt a weight leave my head as the domed green houses faded away. Mother and Father shot me quickly out of the atmosphere.

Bright white lights burst forth all around, blinding me. I'd never known such brightness. I shielded my eyes with one hand. I squeezed the ring of spiders that formed a steering wheel. My vision warbled and turned static. The white murmur of an impending seizure blossomed in my head, into voices from the past. The voices exploded in a succession of hot flashes. My brain stretched into a jellied rope a million miles long, and then it snapped. The bright lights were killing me.

I raced toward the lights. I needed to avoid them, but there was nowhere else to turn.

The fit came on.

My body fought against the seatbelt. I fought against myself to keep control.

I won control.

I terminated the fit before it turned bad.

I won.

I uncovered my eyes and pressed the spider button that engaged the pickled loudspeaker. I held down the button and spoke into a special rigged-up chowder can. My voice projected for miles. The pickled scientists insisted that voices went unheard in outer space, but scientists were too sad to complete their experiments most of the time. Scientists knew nothing of outer space.

I held the empty can to my lips and said, "Bright lights, are you happiness?"

I was approaching the lights at an incredible speed. Eyes and mouths appeared on each of the bright lights, as if they were yawning back to life. They appeared lumpy and misshapen. They had arms and long tails. My rocket ship thrummed forth.

I tried again. "Bright lights, are you happiness?" I

pressed another button to slow the ship. I wiped drool from my mouth.

"Bright lights, are you happiness?"

"We are not happiness," they said. "We are ghosts in a black field. We serve no special function. We cannot help you and we cannot let you pass."

A shiver ran through me. I sweated brine. "If you can't let me pass, can you tell me where to find happiness?"

"Happiness isn't something a pickle has ever gone looking for," they said. "We cannot let you do that. You are a disease. You will destroy everything."

"I'm tired of Pickled Planet. I'm tired of sadness. I just want something else, anything."

I hovered a short distance from the ghosts now.

"What makes you think something better exists? What makes you think happiness didn't go extinct?"

"It's a feeling I have," I said. "I feel something out here calling to me. I deserve to find out who or what is calling. I deserve happiness. I deserve to have it all."

"That is why you cannot have it. You cannot have it all. Now turn around and return to your planet. Quick, before you infect us. We are sad enough from observing your race at a distance."

I loosened my grip on the spider wheel. The lights dimmed, closing the mental window through which convulsions passed. Maybe most pickles gave up so easily, but these ghosts were silly to underestimate me. I had equipped my ship with garlic guns in case a situation like this arose.

My hands depressed the gun triggers, blasting two flurried streams of hungry garlic spiders at the giant ghosts.

"Out of my way, spirits!"

The spiders burrowed into their flesh. Part of me wanted to stick around to see their ghostly organs float away on the dark tracts of space, but I felt that my time was limited.

I sped past them as they clawed holes in themselves. They tore spiders from their wounds and howled at me to stop the feeding.

"Out of my way, spirits."

When I got back on my way, trails of white blood followed me for miles.

Beyond the ship, everything turned monotone. I wouldn't call it darkness. It was less than that. A blankness.

I turned on autopilot and closed my eyes.

Outer space was a downer. I feared that I would never cross another being, let alone a planet.

I had no way to chart the passing of time. Nothing around me felt real. Whenever my insides grumbled, I scarfed a can of cold brine chowder, but being all alone with nothing to do, I became aware of chowder's proclivity for stimulating my most depressing thoughts. I was eating the concentrated essence of my home planet straight from a can. When I framed it this way, I realized brine chowder could jeopardize my entire mission.

I went on a fast. I resolved to eat nothing until I found happiness. I felt less depressed after I stopped eating, but the boredom and solitude of outer space took their toll on me as well. Without food matter in my belly or any room to walk around in my tiny ship, I grew rotten. My skin dried up. A fever came on. My throat itched. Nausea. Aching spine. The ailments piled on until I forced myself to eat another can of chowder. Brine stimulated sadness and sadness was integral to my biology. Deprived of sadness, I was not even myself.

At some point in my fevered daze, I opened my eyes, expecting to look out at more blankness, but the blankness had faded. My rocket ship was nose-diving into a bubbling golden sphere.

Autopilot had failed. I was dead.

HOW THE SUN DIED AT THE DECEITFUL HANDS OF ONE PICKLE

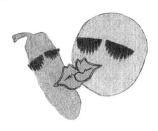

My rocket ship bobbed on the waves of a golden sea. I was lucky my rocket ship remained afloat. Who knew what sea beasts lurked in these waters?

The air smelled sweet.

A big, flat, round, doughy thing in the sky whistled a cheerful melody.

"I am the sun," it said.

This whistling sun worried me. The sun of Pickled Planet never whistled. She shouted curses and death threats. She whispered notes of discouragement. Even stranger than this sun's whistling: its mustache. The sun's bushy brown mustache curled upward at the corners. I wondered why the sun didn't shave the silly thing off. Nobody could take a mustached sun seriously.

Oh drat, I was being a cynic again. I had to stop. I would never unchain myself from the Eternal Plight if I held fast to my prejudices and bad habits. I stuck a hand in the ocean and raised a liquid glob. I brought it to my lips, stuck out my pickled tongue, and took a lick. Sweetness!

I slurped down three handfuls of the ocean and rubbed my hands all over myself. The golden liquid's sweet odor masked my stench of brine. Warm fuzzies tingled in my belly.

"Excuse me," I said. "What is this ocean made of? What is this place and will I find happiness here? Are there beasts in these waters or am I safe to swim ashore?"

The sun's black pupils swung downward in the huge white sockets that housed them. The dark pupils fixed on me. "Pleasant to have a strange traveler today," said the sun, speaking in a baritone voice that rippled the surface of the sea. "Welcome to Pancake Island, the happiest place in the whole wide universe, the final refuge of pancakes against the sadness that has swallowed everything. Nothing in the syrup sea will harm you, but no reason to go ashore either. The bacon vultures will fix your vessel. You will go off soon."

"If this is the happiest place in the universe, can't I stay and be happy?"

"You cannot stay. You are not a pancake."

"That's unfair. Who are these pancakes to horde their privileges? Why can't I have some of their happiness?"

"Pancakes are happy creatures. There is not enough happiness remaining. There is not enough to squander it on those who are not pancakes. As sun and guardian of Pancake Island, it is my duty to fetch help for stranded travelers and send them on their way. We must preserve our way of life. We must preserve happiness. Without us, the universe would be a sad place for everyone."

"The universe *is* a sad place for everyone," I said. "Everyone but you, and you're just a mean old silly sun."

"I am not old or mean. I'm as happy as can be. Everything makes me happy, for I am a pancake."

"Okay," I said, as if in agreement. I was a born deceiver. I would wait for a chance to strike. "Okay, send in your bacon vultures and I'll fly back to my sad planet. I apologize for any inconvenience I may have caused."

"That's more like it. Keep up the polite attitude and

maybe someday you'll experience a greater glimpse of happiness than you received on this temporary landing. Happiness and sadness are not eternal, you know."

"I am from Pickled Planet. My race suffers from the Eternal Plight of the Pickle. Happiness might be ephemeral, but sadness is eternal. I am certain of the latter. Even when sad things die, they keep on being sad. We have no reason for being or not being. We just go on getting worse."

"I am the sun and the gatekeeper, the only pancake aware that poor creatures like you . . ." the sun paused, looked around, sank toward the sea, and whispered in a low voice, his mustache tickling my ear, ". . . *commit suicide.*"

An awkward tension settled between us. I knew the sun was just finishing his statement and wanted no one else to overhear him, but his cold, commanding tone gave the impression that the he was also suggesting that I commit suicide. I wondered why the sun would have it in for me. Was meanness the natural state even of happy suns? Was it the mustache?

"*Suicide,*" the sun whispered.

My face was buried in his mustache.

"Stop breathing on me and summon your vultures. Your mustache tickles."

"*Suicide.*"

"Why are you saying that?"

"*It's my favorite bad word.*"

Maybe I had a reason to be paranoid. Maybe the sun was a pickled pedophile disguised as a pancake. Maybe Pancake Island was not a happy place at all.

"*I only get a chance to say bad words when sad travelers crash here. Pancakes know no bad words. They only know good ones. My proximity to the sky and role as guardian has allowed me to pick up certain words and ideas, things*

I overhear from outer space, things I hear from those like yourself. I like to say bad words. I like to say 'suicide.' It is my favorite word to say.

"*I am never allowed to say it. I am never allowed to talk about it because the pancakes I interact with on a day to day basis would not know what I am talking about. So I am saying it to you, my sorry pickle. You who are unworthy. You who are a disease. The words for who and what you are, for your condition of being, do not exist in this culture. You cannot stay here because as far as pancakes are concerned, sadness does not exist. You do not exist.*"

The sun floated back to a higher point in the sky. I raised my fists toward his golden, fluffy body. I shook my fists and yelled, "I am a pickle! I exist!"

"Oh, I know you exist," the sun said, "but you belong with other pickles, with your sadness. Go home to Pickled Planet. Return and suffer with your species."

I hung my head and rubbed my eyes and sobbed. Real briny tears came out, but the tears were false. As a pickle, I could cry on demand. They were part of my plan, and so far, everything had gone accordingly.

The sun opened his mouth and yawned, as if bored with me. Birds without feathers or bones flapped out of his mouth. Birds of red flesh and white fat. Corpuscular birds with beaks and claws of white fat. Eyes that rolled and melted because they were also made of fat. They must have been the bacon vultures.

They circled my rocket ship several times, descending lower with each succeeding circle, until they landed. They communicated by clapping their crispy wings together. They got busy fixing the rocket ship. They had a stupid way of fixing it, slapping it here and licking it in other places, letting their grease soak in. Since they lived inside the sun, the bacon vultures must have overheard our conversation, but watching them work, I realized that it did not matter. These birds were idiots. They did not understand our mode of speech. I lamented that my ship was likely lost forever, but it hardly mattered since I had no intention of leaving Pancake Island.

I stopped crying. I laughed, pretending to have gotten over the foul mood that had taken hold of me.

I knew I probably caught the strange sensation from drinking those handfuls of the sea, but I figured I might as well query the matter.

"Excuse me," I said. "I drank some of this sea and feel rather pleasant. What is this stuff?"

"This is maple syrup," the sun said. "To prove that I'm a kind sun who sends all voyagers merrily on their way, you may leave with one jar of maple syrup scooped from our tiny sea."

"Just one jar?" I said.

"One jar," the sun said. "Maple syrup is the most important resource in the universe. Without it, our happiness wouldn't be as sweet. It would be nothing at all. Maple syrup is also a very limited resource. The sweetest things always come to an end. We pancakes rejoice in their temporal state. This is one reason we live happy lives. Unlike you, we believe in no eternity. For a while we will be the proprietors of happiness, but no one can say for how long. We've already lost so much. The last agave apes curled up and fell asleep some while ago. They never woke again. The honey horses went before them. Now these creatures sleep on the bottom of the sea, beneath your broken vessel as we speak. No one disturbs the horses and apes, for sleep is a happy thing."

"You're telling me dead animals sleep in the sea of happiness?"

"Dead animals sleep in every sea.

"Happiness slows the decay process, but happy things also break down. They just break down slower. Everything breaks down. It's a matter of when and how bad. When you're happy, breaking down is pleasant. At the peak of psychosomatic breakdown, pancakes dance into the sea. They dissolve into Yummy Decay.

"What is Yummy Decay?"

"It is like being subject and object all at once. The boundaries between your perceptions and the world disintegrate. Pancakes treat Yummy Decay with the greatest deference. Yummy Decay is a state reached only by enlightened pancakes who have lived very long lives. Nobody talks about Yummy Decay. It's just something that happens. The best things in life are never talked about. If there were words to explain them, they would cease being the best things in life. Yummy Decay is too great for words. The awesomeness of Yummy Decay shrugs away all words, like syrup off a bacon vulture's back."

The bacon vultures flapped their wings and took flight from my rocket ship. They squawked ugly grease noises. I hoped they had completed the repairs. Otherwise I was out of luck and might find myself in trouble with the sun.

"I think it's time you leave. We don't want you in our lives," the sun said.

The hairs of his mustache bristled, quivering as if they were tiny fists flailing. My chance was now or never.

I pressed several spider buttons. The cinders of Father and Mother coughed. The rocket ship came alive. I rose up and took pursuit of the bacon vultures. I blasted them with garlic spiders. Hot out of the guns, the spiders melted the fat of the birds. The spiders lost their footing in the melted fat and were carried away by the toasty wind like eight-legged leaves. The birds fared no better. The birds' meat splashed into the sea. Their fat congealed on the golden surface and bobbed there.

I turned the steering wheel for a head-on collision with the sun. I closed my eyes to protect myself from the light. When I opened them again, the rocket ship hit the sun's mustache, tore a green hole through his face, and left him floating in the sky, dead and flecked with brine.

I set my course for shore.

PRIMITIVES ON PARADE

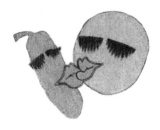

I stepped out of my rocket ship into a bustle of parading pancakes. I had failed to land in a secluded area as hoped, but that was alright. I'd pickled the sun and made my way ashore.

I couldn't yet tell whether to classify the warm feelings inside me as happiness. On a sliding scale, this was certainly the least sad I had ever felt. I reserved any hope I might have. Who knew what these shore-dwelling pancakes would do to me if they discovered that I'd tricked their sun.

I dragged my rocket ship behind me. The ship split the dancing crowd of pancakes. Some of them rode bicycles and unicycles. Others waved to me and called things like "Cheers!" and "Happy breakfast!" and "Awesome bike!"

I presumed they mistook my rocket ship for a bicycle. I resisted frowning. I even smiled and waved, "Thank you!"

I left my rocket ship behind and joined their parade.

The pancakes wore identical maple smiles. The syrup was hard, fixing their expressions and imposing on their flapjack faces the pursed visage of ventriloquists. Their mouths never moved when they spoke. Their hair flowed like pickled fries without the gloom sauce. Their sun-crisped tresses emitted cheer. Their round plump bodies brought ticklish sensations to my groin. I felt naked and ashamed in my slender, warted body.

Their eyes were made of maple, frozen in their sockets.

I wondered what was in those heads of theirs. Were they as empty as they put on? I was afraid of these pancakes. Besides the sun, they were the first happy creatures I had seen. Pancakes on parade could not be the happiest creatures in the universe, but I could be no judge of happiness.

This parade took us through a spud-lined street. It came as a surprise for these pancakes to accept me and allow me to join their parade as if I wasn't just some bitter green monster. I leaned in close to a pancake to my right and keeping with the rhythm of the dancing crowd, I asked, "What are we parading for? Has someone died?"

Funerals were the only parades I had ever taken part in, and on Pickled Planet, the processions were always led by the deceased pickle for whom the funeral was held. Funerals left me severely depressed about the futility of dying. Fortunately, I'd learned from Father and Mother that to get out of a funeral parade, all you had to do was act bedridden. Sometimes we exploited our depression for personal convenience. Sometimes, Mother and Father told me, you won't feel sad enough. Fake your sadness whenever you don't feel sad. Your sadness will always return. Even in our most sincere moments, we pickles were never truly ourselves.

I repeated my question because the pancake failed to hear me over the ruckus of its thousand stampeding fellows.

"The sun has turned a new color," the pancake said. "We are celebrating its old beauty, its new beauty, and all the beautiful forms yet to come. I love the beauty of the sun."

"I love it too," I said. I'd never said I loved anything aloud, and here I was, saying I loved the celestial body I had murdered.

The pancake grabbed me by the hand. Unaccustomed to feeling the touch of another, I jerked my hand away. The pancake stared at its hand, surprised in equal measure, perhaps, that I'd refused its touch, and also that its fingers had turned green.

"I am a mirror of the sun's beauty," the pancake said. "This is the best parade ever."

"How often do you hold parades?" I said, wanting to distract the pancake from noticing that I was also green—and that my touch was responsible for its pickled hand.

"Every day. Every day there is a wonderful parade. Don't you go to all the parades?"

I said that I did, catching sight in that moment of a monolithic green castle and a pancake girl standing atop. She was releasing balloons into the sky. I fell a little bit in love. Without having even met her. I stood in the middle of the street. I wiped briny tears from my eyes and gazed at the pancake in the green castle. My heart yawned, stretched, and began to thump, awaking from a very long coma.

After overcoming the initial shock of not feeling dead inside for the first time in my life, I moved on with the parade, to a feast on the other side of Pancake Island.

The potato housing district ended.

We climbed a hill that peaked in the center of the island. The hill was a pancake. In the center of the peak, a fountain spewed syrup. The pancakes got down on their knobby knees and ladled syrup from the fountain. The syrup rolled down their chins. It seeped in through their porous flesh and made them glow.

I pushed my way into their circle and drank syrup from the fountain. Sometimes pancakes raised their heads and wiped their mouths and smiled or cheered.

Other pancakes drank from crystalline bottles. "What's in the bottles?" I asked the pancake to my left.

"Fanny Fod's maple beer. It's the most delicious beer ever."

"Who's Fanny Fod?"

"The pancake in the green castle."

"Oh," I said, lowering my head to the fountain.

I drank syrup until my belly bloated and I collapsed. I lay there, not thinking much about anything.

Eventually, I got up. I patted my full belly and separated myself from the parade. I headed for the green castle, leaving a trail of pickled footprints in my wake.

I COME KNOCKING AT YOUR DOOR

The green castle was tall and narrow. I walked across a yard of blooming pancake flowers. I knocked on the green door.

Knock knock.
Knock.

The green door opened quick, as if she had been standing on the other side, watching me through the peephole.

"Hi," the pancake said.
"My name is Gaston Glew."
"My name is Fanny W. Fod."
"I'm sorry if this is awkward."
"It's not awkward."
We laughed nervously.
"We are sharing a first moment," she said.
"This is good," I said. "My life has been one long trail of snot and boogers. How about yours?"
"You're not from around here."
"I come from Pickled Planet."
"How did you get past the sun? A few times in my life I have seen foreign travelers enter our atmosphere, but the sun always sends them on their way."
"Oh, the sun and I cut a deal. I agreed to trim his mustache every morning in exchange for citizenship."

"The sun was kind to cut you a deal. The sun never cuts a deal with anyone. He must have sensed you were special."

"Yeah, I guess."

"Do you have a place to stay on Pancake Island?"

"I arrived a few hours ago."

"You must have arrived when the sun turned green. The sun must have really liked you to change colors. Maybe he wanted to cheer you up. Would you like to come into my kitchen? Here, come on."

"Okay." I followed her into the kitchen.

She told me to sit on one of the potato chairs surrounding a pancake table.

There was a pawing and a scratching and a slapping at the back door.

"The Cuddlywumpus senses your sadness," she said. She lowered her eyes and made an embarrassed facial expression. We were sliding into the pit of an awkward situation.

"Cuddlywumpus?" I said. "Is that what's at the door?"

"No, Nothing," she said. "It's Nothing."

The Nothing howled. It made a sound like "Ra-ra roo! Ra-ra roo!" over and over again.

"That is more than Nothing," I said. "I know what Nothing sounds like. This thing is more than Nothing and it's unhappy."

"Unhappy? This is Pancake Island. Nothing is unhappy."

The thing on the other side of the door sounded more upset now that we were talking about it. Nobody likes to overhear others talking about them. This was always the case on Pickled Planet, although none of us ever changed. We turned even sadder when we heard other pickles complaining about our sadness, saying things like, *"What is wrong with Gaston Glew? He did not do what he was sup-*

posed to do today." "What was he supposed to do today?" "He was supposed to attend a funeral." "Did you attend a funeral?" "No, but I am superior to Gaston Glew and am therefore exempt from any blame." "You are right, we must hold Gaston Glew accountable for the grievous error that is his life. We must punish him." "He thinks we will let him off the hook." "Let us punish him twice as bad for being twice as sad as us and thinking we will let him off the hook." "Let us punish him for not being sad enough." "We have such sadness to show him." Mutual sighs. "Gaston Glew is a loser."

"You need to leave," she said.

The psychic debris cleared from my mind. Some anxious crumbs of thought floated across my vision. I raised my eyebrows, trying to look shocked and indignant. The Nothing in the cellar was screaming now. The Nothing in the cellar could not tolerate the presence of a creature as sad as myself.

I lowered my eyebrows and scrunched my forehead, as if puzzled, even though I knew exactly what was going on, perhaps more than she did. "What did I do?" I said. "I just felt a little distracted. Don't you get distracted?"

"Pancakes are too happy in each moment to consider anything a distraction."

"Doesn't that mean everything is a distraction?"

She turned around and motioned for me to follow her.

"Are you kicking me out?"

"You can't stay here, so leave. Go anywhere."

"But we've only just met. I'm attracted to you, Fanny Fod. It's you who called me to this place, not happiness."

"You should explore your options. I am just a pancake. Happiness is happier than all the happy pancakes combined. You've upset the Nothing. I think it's neat that you match my castle, but I can't let you ruin my life."

"You owe me a chance."

"Get out of my castle."

"You'll come to regret this."

"How can I regret anything? I'm happy by myself. Plus, I don't even know you."

"Fine, I'll leave," I said, "if you show me your Nothing first."

Blue tears welled up in her blueberry eyes as she began to cry. "Leave before the Cuddlywumpus dies. It senses your sadness. The Cuddlywumpus is everything to me."

I should have tried to comfort her. I raised my voice instead. "What is this Cuddlywumpus? You told me there was a Nothing. A Cuddlywumpus is more than Nothing. You're a liar. How can it sense my sadness? There is no sadness on Pancake Island. There is no sadness anymore inside my--"

"Get out! Your sadness is killing the Cuddlywumpus!"

She lost her composure. Like a pickle, she lost control.

"Fine, I'll leave you with your beast," I said. I turned and left through the zucchini door.

As I marched across the lawn, my footsteps left briny indentations in the ground. Pancake flowers near my dead footprints raised their heads, choked up greenish black syrup and collapsed in their own bile, like the cacti back home used to do.

The dead sun spit green phlegm across the horizon. I looked up at him and felt bad for what I'd done. I'd been on Pancake Island for half a day at most and I had caused a lot of damage. I hadn't even thought much about what I planned to do here. I had not achieved the full happiness experience, but already I questioned whether that was what I truly sought. These pancakes obviously enjoyed themselves, but if all they did was feast and party every day, well, that was not really what I desired. I wanted to feel airy and relaxed forever, but maybe the sun was right. Maybe I was better off climbing into my rocket ship and heading back to Pickled Planet. Obviously I did not belong. It was probably better not to disturb these happy creatures any more than I already had.

But this pancake in the green castle, she seemed different than the rest. She seemed like someone I might be able to talk to. Just seeing her releasing balloons over the island made me want to climb up there and live forever in the castle with her. Despite the prospect of discovering even more enchanting pancakes on this island, and maybe getting to the root of happiness, I had lost my desire to explore. I'd found what I came for, and I was going to make her see that I hadn't traveled halfway across the universe to be happy. I had traveled halfway across the universe to find her.

I turned around and marched up to her front door again. She was going to hear me out. She was going to learn all about the Eternal Plight of the Pickle and how she could cure me with her love.

Knock knockknock knock, knock.
Knock. Knock.
Knock, knockknock . . . knock, knock . . .
Knockknockknock.
KNOCK. KNOCK. KNOCK.
KNOCKKNOCKKNOCKKNOCKKNOCK--

"Hey, what're you doin' there?" someone shouted, disturbing my knocking.

I turned around. The shouter was a pancake.

"I'm a door inspector. I inspect doors," I said, and regretted saying it. I was on a mission. I could not let myself get distracted. Anyway, who knew if door inspectors existed on Pancake Island?

"Fanny Fod has a good door, doesn't she?" the pancake said.

I was tempted to tell the pancake to bug off and return to my knocking, to rejoinder it this time with shouted professions of love, but I realized I had already crossed the line, banging on her door for an inordinate duration. The pancake was right, though. Fanny Fod had a good door.

"Have you tested my door yet?" the pancake said.

Having returned to myself and seeing the fool I'd been, I decided to play nice for a little bit. This pancake knew Fanny Fod's name. I could dig into this pancake for more information. "I don't know. Where do you live? I'm offering free inspections all day."

The pancake giggled and shrugged as if I had said something very silly. "In my potato. Where else?"

I raised a tired arm and pointed at the sky. "Lead the way and I'll inspect your door with twice as many knocks as I gave this one."

"You're so kind, Mr. Door Inspector."

I put on a fake smile and hoped to end this soon.

The pancake took my hand and led me away from Fanny Fod's castle. I turned and looked behind me, hurting inside because I felt Fanny's blueberry eyes watching me. I probably looked like the biggest jerk, allowing this other pancake to take me away under the guise of being a door inspector only moments after trying to break down her door and say I loved her, even though we had just met.

"How do you feel, Mr. Door Inspector?" the pancake said.

"Um . . ."

"Um is a good way to feel. I am happy you feel um. Do you want to know how I feel?"

"I guess so."

"I feel happy. I feel liberated. I feel . . . excited."

"Do you feel that way all the time?"

"Of course. I am always glad. Are you glad?"

"I am glad."

"You don't sound glad."

"I am glad."

"It's funny that I should find a door inspector today. I was staring at my door for a long time yesterday and it was so fascinating. I thought a door inspector must inspect my door. Any door inspector who inspects my door will love it. I can't wait for you to love my door. It's a fascinating door. I sometimes miss the Ultra Yummy Happiness Parade because I can't pull myself away from the door. Sometimes I miss many parades in a row. I stare at my door for days, basking in the good door vibes. I think my door is a bunch of pancakes that fell so in love they became one pancake and they're always making love, having one constant stream of orgasms. When I'm not around my door, I like to think my door misses me. I like to think my door has orgasms in my absence."

I blocked out the pancake's door babble. I could stand no more. What was I doing here? This pancake only cared about finding happiness in her door. I only cared about finding happiness in Fanny Fod.

We walked through a field of pancake flowers that'd sprung up out of nowhere. The flowers turned green and pickled in my wake. The flowers frowned like ugly mirrors. I hated myself for killing them. Holding hands with this strange pancake, I calculated that I would hate myself for approximately forever. It was my duty as a sufferer of the Eternal Plight to hate myself. I mouthed the motto of Captain Pickle. *Unchain yourself from this briny fate, oh pickled prisoner!* But Captain Pickle wasn't real. He was make-believe. I did not share the privilege of being imaginary. None of us did, no matter how hard we tried.

"The flowers love you," the pancake said. "They are remaking themselves in your image."

Okay, maybe this pancake could teach me something about happiness. Maybe all pancakes were obsessed and in love with one thing and that one thing was the wellspring of all their happiness and maple syrup was what enabled them to love. Without maple syrup, they would be as sad as I was. Now the syrup had worked through me and I was in love and almost happy, but love had turned me crazy as a door creep. Now that I had experienced a little taste of happiness, I could remain neither happy nor sad.

Unchain yourself from this briny fate, oh pickled prisoner!

I walked behind her, up some steps carved into a giant potato. I was about to say something negative, out of habit, but I resisted. I had to act like a door inspector. Father was a door inspector. I just had to act like Father. We stopped on a stoop outside a brown and knotted potato door. The stoop was small. We pressed together. I considered stepping down to the stair beneath to put some distance between us, but the pancake wrapped her arms around me. She stared at me with unmoving maple eyes. "Do you like my door?" she said, her mouth unmoving. Stiff.

"I love it," I said. I couldn't look at her any longer. I couldn't look at the door either. I envisioned pushing her down the stairs and shouting, "Your door is boring! I hate your door!" I could rip the door from its weak root hinges and toss it down on top of her and kill her. I would not do that. That would be inappropriate.

"Kiss me," the pancake said.

I kissed her. I didn't know what else to do.

"Come on. The inside of the door is more interesting than the outside."

I kissed her again. Her lips were like a maple lollipop that happened to be attached to a living creature. It mattered little whether I cared for this pancake, or whether she cared for me. We'd made a silent agreement not to care about each other. Tasting her, I decided that I might enjoy her company in spite of my best intentions.

"Come on," she pleaded. "I want you to see the inside."

She turned away from me and opened the door and walked inside. "This will end badly," I mumbled.

"What?" she said.

"Nothing," I said, and followed her into the potato house to learn the wonders of her crappy door, and maybe suck on her lips a little.

Oh Fanny Fod, I thought, I'm sorry.

I entered her potato and closed the door behind me.

Beyond the potato door, the beloved object of this pancake whom I shortly expected to screw in exchange for information, a mountain of doors greeted me. Each potato door squirmed against the other doors.

Red gravy bled from the doors.

The house was wet and smelled like bleach.

"Don't you love my door?" the pancake said.

"Well . . . it's not just one door. It's many doors, and none of them are connected to the door that leads outside."

The pancake laughed at me. "Oh, you're silly. All doors are connected."

"Maybe, perhaps." I had to act like a door inspector, like I knew what I was doing. "But what are potato doors doing on Pancake Island? What do potatoes have to do with pancakes and doors?" I had failed to find the right moment to ask these questions until now.

The pancake did not question why I was unaware of facts that must have been common knowledge to all pancakes. She was that oblivious. She told me a pretty good story the pancakes told each other about their castles. The story went that once upon a time, a long time ago, there lived a race of pancakes who were made out of potatoes. They decided to evolve for some reason or another and died in their potato forms to reincarnate as hip, happy, modern day pancakes. That is why so many potato castles sprouted up in the syrup-rich soil of Pancake Island. According to the story, there was an even older race of pancakes: the zucchini race. Zucchini pancakes did not exist for very long. Some believed that the zucchini pancakes migrated from Pancake Island for one reason or another. Fanny Fod lived in the only zucchini castle left alive.

"So how about it?" the pancake said.

"How about what?"

"Are you going to inspect my door or what?"

"I said I loved it."

"That's not your full inspection, is it?"

"Let me see."

I circled the mountain of doors, occasionally leaning over and making a ticking noise with my tongue, pretending to be deep in thought. I ran my fingers along the edge of several doors and everywhere my fingers touched, turned green. That really impressed the pancake. "Yes," she said. "It needed that extra flair."

"Leave it to a door expert," I said.

I walked around the door mountain three times in all, stroking it here and there, gesticulating ambivalently at times to suggest that I had not yet made up my mind about her door.

"What is it?" she said.

"I'm not sure. Something's missing. Do you think . . . let me rephrase that. Do you know what a Cuddlywumpus is?"

Her body swayed back and forth horizontally,

indicating a negative. "A Cuddlywumpus? I've never heard of such a thing."

"Do you think *Cuddlywumpus* might be the name of a door?"

"It could be, but it has never occurred to me to name my door."

I was relieved to hear that. It would be a huge letdown if the mysterious Cuddlywumpus turned out to be nothing more than a talking door. I might even lose all interest in Fanny Fod if I discovered that she obsessed herself over a door. "Do you think you could inspect me now?" the pancake said.

I knew it. I knew she wanted something else from me. No matter how much she loved her door, she had insisted on my visitation for a different reason right from the start. The mountain of doors was only a pretext. Everything boiled down to a lot of door nonsense.

"Well can you?" She twitched like a squashed insect.

"What can you offer me in return?"

"There are no returns on happiness," she said.

She stepped toward me. I raised my arms to defend myself but she was not trying to attack. She fell at my feet. Her flat round body heaved. "Please inspect me, Mr. Door Inspector," she said.

"Get off the floor."

"Join me on the floor."

"Fine." I got down beside her on the floor.

She threw her arms around me. She pressed her maple lips to mine and said, "There are no returns on happiness."

"I don't know what you mean," I said.

"All I mean is what I say."

I licked her lips as she dragged her palms down my green belly, under the elastic band of my yellow spacesuit pants.

I thereafter became aroused.

The pancake cooed softly as she stroked my little pickle. I sucked on her lips. No matter how many mouthfuls of her sweet face I sucked away, she remained whole. She existed in a perpetual cycle of pleasure and replenishment. Her happiness reserves ran deep, extending far beyond her physical body. I considered the possibility that love had fostered in her a psychic connection with the doors, a stockpile of happy feelings.

I laughed to myself. I was quick to figure out others, and quick to fault them for being so easy to figure out.

Now I had to follow through with the act, to have sex with the pancake, to inspect her, as it were.

While these thoughts distracted me, pulling me farther inside myself and numbing me to the outside world, she removed my spacesuit. My little pickle was stiff. I had never seen it fully erected, being too depressed for that and never meeting any pickles I was attracted to, but erect, my little pickle was longer than me. It was much skinnier, though. In fact, my little pickle looked a lot like Father.

The pancake pulled away from me. She ran her mouth up the shaft of my little pickle. She grabbed hold of it, swung herself around, and wound up on top of me, straddling my chest. We were completely naked.

"How is this going to work?" I said.

"Be patient," she said. "You have to inspect other parts of me before you inspect the inside."

"Yes, but it is going to be very difficult to inspect your insides when the time comes if I am not sure how to apply my inspection rod."

"No need to worry. The door will help us."

The front door trembled on its hinges, opened into a mouth, and burst into spasms of laughter.

"The door senses that you will inspect me soon. That

is why we must go slow. The door will help us when the time comes, and the longer it takes to set off our pleasure buttons, the happier the door will be."

I tuned the radio antenna of my mind to a sweet station where our lips came together for hours, and as long as we stayed very still, and kissed very quietly, and used only the muscles used for kissing, worried thoughts no longer harried me. And I didn't have to feel bad about Fanny Fod, or angry that the front door was laughing at me.

Sometime later she pulled away. She said, "That is enough of that. It is time to inspect other parts now." She moved her body forward, planting her pancake crotch right over my face.

I flailed my arms. I was suffocating. I could not swallow the maple syrup filling my throat.

"Breathe through me. My flesh is porous," she said.

I opened my mouth. Syrup poured out, unclogging my esophagus. Her pancake body reabsorbed the syrup. Her pores split open into soft little urchin mouths. Each one of her pores suckled my face as she gyrated. The mouths expanded. They became so large they grew into each other until all the tiny mouths lost themselves in one giant mouth.

The mountain of doors disassembled. The doors waddled, slithered, and floated. They came to surround us. A few of them ignored us in favor of the front door. Those doors wasted no time engaging the front door in acts that, from the sounds they made, gratified their sexual desires.

The doors that surrounded us took hold of the pancake. She quivered and moaned, dissolving into a joy that called to mind, in its physical manifestations, a pickle seized by epilepsy. The doors pulled her off of me and pinned her to the floor. They spread her wide as if to rape her. Syrup oozed down the puffy wedge of her snatch. She quivered and moaned. My brain tingled.

"Come with me," she said.

Lying beside her in this way, I felt giddy and awkward.

"What? Come where?" I said.

The doors' knobs slinked outward into rubbery, snakelike poles.

"Come have fun with me, Mr. Door Inspector," she said.

"I don't know how to have fun," I said. It was true. I'd never had fun in my entire life.

"Come inspect me, then."

Several doors raised me to my feet. Two more grabbed hold of my little pickle and guided it into the pancake's dripping crotch.

We engaged in the awful activity that followed for approximately twice the time it takes to hang oneself. All the while, I thought of better things I could have been doing, like finding a path into the heart of Fanny Fod, the one I truly loved.

At least the doors were able to satisfy themselves. They stroked their knobs as they bore witness to our performance of the esoteric biological ritual. The doors distracted and unnerved me, but at least they did not try to penetrate my pickled anus with their knobs.

Eventually, a splotch of brine was milked from my little pickle and the inspection ended.

I got paranoid. I feared this pancake was in cohorts with her doors to take advantage of me, to use me in some nefarious fashion, something far worse than what had already been done. My little pickle shrank back to nothing.

I stood up. I pushed my way out of the circle of doors

and clenched my fists. I punched at the air. I was sweaty and paranoid, sticky and regretful. I wanted no one around. I could not contain myself much longer.

"Are you happy, Mr. Door Inspector?" the pancake said. "Would you like to inspect me again?"

"No," I shouted, then rescinded. "Okay, but only if we do it my way."

"We can do it any way you like," she said.

I pushed my way back into the circle of doors. I moved to the center and lay down on top of her.

The pancake squirmed beneath me.

My little pickle remained flaccid.

"I'm so glad," she said. "Are you glad?"

I opened my mouth to speak. I looked at the doors around me. I could not answer her question. I could no longer tolerate this insulting audience.

"Are you glad?" she repeated.

I responded with a head butt that broke her face apart. Her syrupy brains oozed out, and that was that. The pancake was dead.

She turned green and stiff beneath me.

My little pickle lengthened, throbbing and alert.

"Are you glad?" I asked the corpse.

I forced myself inside her and gave her a final go.

With a dead partner, I almost enjoyed the act.

I stood again, ready to fight the doors if they tried to attack. They stroked themselves, staring blankly. I staggered toward the open front door. A writhing pack of other doors groped and sucked its knob.

I fled.

DEATH OF A HUMP CHILD

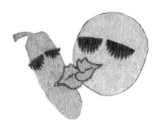

I ran from the house of doors. It was night now and I did not know where I was going or what I was doing or why I had murdered the pancake and if a pancake police force existed and if they did exist would they track me down and how did pancakes treat killers? I ran without knowing where I was going, but I had to get away all the same. I could not stay there. I could not stay anywhere. I had to find my rocket ship.

I ran down a street. Potato houses towered overhead. Pop music shrieked through the air. Pancakes leaned out the windows and danced in the yards and waved to me as I passed. "Come join us," they said. "We're having so much fun."

No you're not, I thought. You're not having any fun. You just think you're having fun, but you've been conned. You all think you're happy because you're drugged all the time.

"Happiness is real, real is happiness," they said, as if reading my thoughts. I was under psychic attack.

I dashed past so many dancing pancakes. They moved like marionettes controlled by clumsy, trembling hands.

I felt I'd run down this street for my entire life, until it finally ended. The gleeful shouts and pop music died.

The street ended at the shore. I collapsed in the shallow

lap of waves and closed my eyes. My burning lungs began to cool. I opened my eyes and looked upward, expecting the sad moon of Pickled Planet, but the night was moonless. The sun stayed visible, green. Like all green things, the sun was dead. Its glow streaked the pancake shore. I followed the glow with my eyes, then sprang up, aghast at what I saw. Not far away, a child pancake was humping an ovular hole dug in the side of my rocket ship.

With a hard, earnest thrust, he threw his arms in the air and shouted, "Wee, oh fun!"

I squatted on all fours like a beast. My body shook. My body emitted a sweet odor, but the scent of syrup was not enough to calm my nerves this time. I would kill the nasty little prick.

The pancake pulled away. His little pancake burped sticky stuff onto the green-lit beach. It was my turn to show him what fun was really about.

He stood there oblivious, stroking the sides of my ship. For the love of decency, I thought, hump something that is alive.

Hypocrite.

Silently, I pounced. Years of feeling invisible to the world had made me as stealthy and agile as any pickle. If sadness hadn't pickled my planet, I could have become what the cucumbers used to call *gymnastics champions*. Imagine that. Gaston Glew, gymnastics champion. Instead, I was killing children on a foreign planet.

I took the pancake child by surprise. I punched my fists through the back of his head and ripped his eyes out of his face. He giggled as he leaked brain.

I guess you could not hurt the really happy ones.

I tossed his eyes into the waves and climbed into my rocket ship. I started it up, then got an idea. I fetched a case of brine chowder and climbed out of the ship.

"Fun for sale," I said. "Who wants fun? This fun comes in many flavors. Fun for sale!"

"Wee, oh fun," the pancake said. Everything in his body had leaked out through his face.

"I want fun," he said.

"How much fun do you want?" I said.

"I would like enough fun for everyone."

"Coming right up," I said. I set down the case of brine chowder and kicked him in the stomach. He doubled over but did not go down. I jerked him straight and leaned in close and bit his nose off. He was the first pancake I'd taken a real bite of. His nose was rich with clotted syrup.

I took a bite from the corner of his mouth, getting a little lip in with the rest because the pancake/maple syrup combination was killer.

I swallowed the piece of his face.

"Are we having fun yet?" I said.

He looked very stupid and surprised with part of his face missing.

I kicked him and this time he fell. He threw his arms to his sides and strained his mouth to cry, "Wee, oh fun!"

"Now lie still," I said.

I took three chowder cans from the case and stomped them into the pancake's belly. I stomped the rest of the cans into him, three at a time. His mouth was pushed so far into the island's surface by the cans, there was no way to know whether he still thought we were having a fun time. When I stepped off of him, all that remained was a perfect circle of half-buried chowder cans. Syrupy blood leaked beyond the circle's perimeter.

I had felt good while killing him, but post-kill, I plummeted back into the dumps. I'd messed up again. There was no justice in revenge. This twerp didn't deserve to die. I could have just made off in my rocket ship. He may have been screwing around with it, but only because he didn't know any better.

"I'm sorry," I said.

It was the first time I'd uttered an apology in my life. Who was I speaking to? More than the mere child. Who then? Father and Mother? The ghosts? The sun and his bacon vultures? The pancake and her doors? I was apologizing to the living as well, to Fanny Fod and others who might someday step into my path and be destroyed forever.

I could not let myself damage things anymore. I was best off blasting away in my rocket ship and living out the sad remainder of my existence alone in outer space, having experienced my pin drop of happiness.

I looked out at the green-tinted syrup sea and wondered, Why must I suffer the Eternal Plight of the Pickle? Why must my heart be full of brine?

I was alone on the beach with the dead pancake child. I felt like I had spent a lot of my life standing next to dead things. I did not like standing next to dead things, so I waded out waist-high into the sea and let the syrup's healing powers soothe me.

After a while, I sloshed my way out of the sea and went straight to my rocket ship. I removed what remained of the brine chowder, tore out the control panel, and detached both rocket boosters. They were still packed with the ashes of Father and Mother.

When the rocket ship was totally empty, I went over to the pancake child's humping hole. I took a deep breathe and sealed my mouth over the hole. It was sticky.

I blew all the air in my lungs into the hump hole. The ship's walls expanded a little, like a balloon. I blew again and again until the ship lifted up, floating a few inches off the island. Encouraged by my progress, I blew into the hole faster, blowing into the hole at a tremendous rate. The ship floated higher, up to my head, then above me. I kept on blowing until the ship was almost out of reach. I jumped and wrapped my arms around it. I slipped inside the rocket-ship-turned-balloon.

I'd removed the controls because it had occurred to me while standing in the sea that a great deal of my unhappiness stemmed from a drive for control. If I wanted to move forward, I had to shed all of that. I had to surrender control. My surrender began with my removal of the steering wheel and ended with my turning the rocket ship into a gigantic balloon.

"You are free to take me anywhere," I told the balloon.

It began to move through the sky.

We floated for a while, then the balloon popped and the air swooshed out. I was trapped inside it, falling through the sky at a screamless velocity, naked and confused.

HAPPY GRIEVANCES

"Hold still, you've gone and hung yourself," said a voice. It was Fanny Fod.

"Where am I?" I called.

"I shot your balloon out of the sky. You were supposed to land on the rooftop, but you veered at the last minute and nearly crashed to your doom. The balloon formed a hand and reached out and grabbed hold of a spire. The hand is holding steady, but I'm afraid it won't stay that way forever. Be very still and don't say a word. I'll have you out of there in no time."

I obeyed, motionless and quiet. In my head, I imagined my brains splattering on the walkway of Fanny Fod's castle. I imagined her scooping my ruined body into her arms and eating me.

Fanny's brow furrowed. "You were wearing a suit earlier," she said.

"Yes, I was."

"Is it gone now because you had a special encounter with a pancake?"

"No," I said. "I have had no special encounters."

"Be honest."

"I am."

"Okay," she said.

"Okay," I said.

It was getting awkward again.

"I apologize for earlier," she said. "For kicking you out. I had reasons to act the way I did, but those reasons don't concern you. Anyway, I was planning to make dinner. Are you hungry?"

"I would like to eat food," I said.

"Let's go inside and eat food," she said.

So we went inside and ate food.

SLEEP TOGETHER

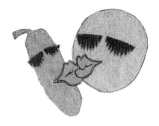

We were sitting at the potato table, full from a pancake dinner. Fanny Fod was lactating beer into a glass. When the glass was full, she lactated into another glass. She added spices and a lot of other things I did not recognize.

"What are we drinking?" I said, taking up the glass she'd passed me. Even though I already knew this was beer, it was best to play dumb.

"Maple beer," she said, raising her glass to her mouth.

"It smells delicious." I refrained from mentioning how excited I was to consume her body fluids. For the moment, I wanted to avoid saying anything awkward. I slurped some beer. It was dark, heavy, sweet.

"Yum," I said.

We focused on our beers for a little while.

"So what's your middle initial stand for?" I asked.

"Winter," she said. "Would you like to hear the story why?"

I said that I would.

"It starts with my mother, Fall M. Fod. Fall was a famous pancakeologist."

The W. in Fanny's name stood for "Winter," the season she was born, and the M. in Fall's name stood for "Monogamy." All pancakes chose their own middle name. Fall chose hers because of a story about a custom that existed in the potato days: monogamy. I knew monogamy caused a lot of pain and misery on Pickled Planet. The difference between pickles and potatoes was that potatoes had learned how to identify and throw out what made them sad, a skill which led them down a supremely happy evolutionary road. Fall embraced monogamy as a lifestyle choice.

As a sign that she followed in the monogamous footsteps of her Mother, and also as a way of letting her individuality show, Fanny chose "Winter" as her middle name. She was the only monogamous pancake and monogamy struck other pancakes as funny.

"That's a good story," I said. I did not feel much like sharing the story behind my middle name. I did not feel much like sharing any stories.

"Can I have another beer?" I said.

"Of course."

She took my glass and milked herself until foam spilled over the lip of the glass. She added no spices this time.

She did not drink another beer.

After I drank the beer, I lowered my head, suddenly tired and wanting to laugh at myself. I'd never eaten dinner naked before. I lifted my head and smiled at her. I twiddled my fingers, looked up at Fanny Fod, my fingers, her.

"Thank you for the food and beer. I would like to eat your face now," I said.

It was an awkward thing to say, but there it was. I'd said it.

She laughed and said, "Let's go to sleep."

I stayed planted in the potato chair. She stood and took me by the hand and guided me out of the kitchen, up a green spiral staircase, and into a curved room. In the center of the room was a translucent, squishy bed filled with syrup. She slipped out of her green dress and we got into bed.

We met in the center of the bed. She folded over me like an umbrella. The pale green night came through the window and made our bodies look as if they were one body, like two ghosts sharing the same sheet. We nuzzled our faces together to complete the illusion.

I opened my mouth to say something but there was nothing to say. This was one of those greatest moments the dead sun told me about. Our touching each other was a thing no words could stomp into the ground.

"Do you have enough blankets?" she said.

"Yes, thank you. What kind of blankets are these?"

"They are crepe blankets."

"I like them."

"Thank you. I made them myself."

She planted her peanut butter lips over my cracked and salty smile.

Our mouths together, we shared a yummy dream.

Fanny Fod and I woke up early the next morning. Syrup fastened our foreheads together. Our limbs were tangled in a comfortable knot.

In one swift motion, she pulled away from me and sat up in bed.

"I like you," she said. "And I appreciate your company, but I'm not just going to fall into your arms. You have to know that."

I sighed. What a turnaround. Was love going to be as hard to maintain as everything else?

"I came all this way," I said. "You were waiting for a sad thing and I came. I'm your sad thing."

"I know that you're sad, but you are not the last sad

creature in the universe. You might be the wrong sad thing for me."

"I can feel it. We're meant for each other, Fanny Fod."

"Gaston Glew, after so many years of feeling wrong in heart and broken in mind, why do you continue following your thoughts and feelings? I've been happy all my life and even I know better than to trust what I think and feel."

"See, right there. There's us being meant for each other. That's not something you would know about me from the short time we've known each other, and I know things I shouldn't know about you. It's unreal. You were calling to me through outer space. The telescopes in our minds were programmed to seek each other out."

"I don't have a telescope in my mind. My head is too flat."

"Okay, fine, anyway, I know I'm right," I said. "I never put trust in anyone, but I trust you already."

"You don't know me."

"I don't know anyone."

"Then it's a choice you've made to trust me, and it sounds to me like you've made a lot of bad decisions in your life. You're being rash."

"I escaped my destined fate to rot away with the rest of the pickles, didn't I?"

"That may have been your worst decision of all."

"There it is again. The psychic connection. You wouldn't make that judgment unless you knew me far beyond anything I've said. Exile was my best decision. I tried to fit in. I tried to be a good pickle. Now that I've experienced this other world, the most terrifying prospect is going back to Pickled Planet, to what I was before."

"What you were is what a part of you will always be."

"I thought you pancakes believed nothing is eternal."

"Most believe it, but I don't." She hesitated for a few breaths, then said, "Are you really happy here?"

"I'm happy. I'm happy and I'm speaking honestly."

"You're speaking honestly?"

"Yes," I said.

"You're speaking honestly?"

"Yes, I think so."

"Okay, if you're speaking honestly, why are you not out trimming the sun's mustache right now? Isn't that where you should be?"

"Oh, that," I said.

"It's okay. You can tell me. Do you also want to tell me if you had any special encounters with any pancakes yesterday? It's okay if you did. It's okay to tell me why you were naked when I shot you out of your balloon."

I cracked up inside. I felt a lot depended on my response. Either way I was doomed.

"Well?" she said.

I was out of space to breathe.

"No, no special encounters," I said.

Fanny pursed her peanut butter lips into a disappointed half-smile that was flecked with syrup. I felt bad about lying to her, but I had other things to worry about. My belly was grumbling. I was hungry. Her face looked so delectable, I wanted to eat her for breakfast. I wanted to flatten her on the bed and eat her.

"I have to go," she said. "Help yourself to anything. Go anywhere. But whatever you do, don't enter the dungeon."

Fanny left the castle to distribute beer around Pancake Island. I drifted back to sleep and slept in later than I had in my entire life. It was a more relaxing sleep than any I'd gotten on Pickled Planet. My sleep there was troubled, full of night tremors and voices telling me to do things in the dark, so I had to sleep with the lights on most nights, if I could fall asleep at all. Most nights I tossed and turned in fear of the faces detached from bodies that I thought were pressing against every window of the house. The faces were not trying to break into the house. They were trying to smother it. I lay awake, holding my breath and sweating brine, waiting for the heads to come for me. Some nights I couldn't take it. I locked myself in the bathroom and wrapped myself around the toilet and cried uncontrollably. I slammed my head against the toilet seat until I lost consciousness and stopped thinking about the faces. Blackouts were my only defense against the fear. Most nights, blacking out was the only way I could rest, and even then I sensed the smothering. My brain lost communication with the rest of my body and I sank through layer after layer of green sand.

And so waking in the morning, feeling alive and rested in someone else's bed, I sprang up, ran to the rooftop, and shouted to the world, "Peace be with you!"

I felt every atom burst in pancake peace and harmony. I wanted to bless everyone.

"Pancake love for all!"

Restful sleep had also invigorated my curiosity, which was perfect because Fanny was out and I had the entire zucchini castle to explore. The starting point was obvious. I'd have to check out the dungeon and see the Cuddlywumpus for myself. It was true that Fanny Fod had kicked me out of her castle after the Cuddlywumpus started howling during our initial encounter, but maybe sleeping together counted as a rite of passage that granted me permission to witness the wonders of the mysterious Cuddlywumpus.

I giggled like a little pancake as I ran back into the castle and took the spiral staircase down to the kitchen. On the counter, Fanny Fod had left me two bottles of beer and a plate of peanut butter pancakes made from her smile. I did a shimmy dance across the kitchen, surprising even myself. It felt good to wake up somewhere you belonged. Even breathing was a pleasant, exciting activity. I popped open a beer, took a sip, ate two pancakes, and rubbed my belly. This was the ultimate breakfast. If every breakfast were a nation, no breakfast in the history of breakfasts could lay a finger on this one. It was a utopian breakfast.

I ate another pancake, rubbed my belly, and polished off the first beer. It was very resourceful of Fanny to use only ingredients from her own body. It was resourceful and she did it well.

I patted my stuffed belly and did a sluggish shimmy. I decided to name this one. I named it The Great and Beautiful Breakfast Empire. I thought maybe I would show it to Fanny Fod when she got home as a thank you for breakfast.

I heard the Cuddlywumpus snuffling behind the dungeon door and decided I should have a look. Fanny never mentioned when she might return. I put my ear to the door. There was a soft, ruffling sound. It sounded like the Cuddlywumpus was right behind the door and I had startled it. "Excuse me," I said, knocking. "May I come in?"

The Cuddlywumpus did not reply. I slowly reached for the doorknob until my hand grasped its green handle. I held my hand there for a while before turning it. Although I failed to see how a pancake as kind and generous and beautiful as Fanny Fod could keep a dangerous pet around, there was the off chance.

Pickles used to keep sad and dangerous pets all the time, not because they had any use for sad and dangerous pets. In our part of the universe, rubber monsters fell out of the sky rather often. When pickles encountered these monsters, they did not know what to do with them, so they put them in soggy boxes and called them pets. They took the rubber monsters home and made them into pets because they did not know what else to do with them, and sometimes the rubber monsters became sad and dangerous pets.

The Cuddlywumpus sounded sad the first day. I felt pretty certain it would not be one of those pets that was sad and dangerous, though. This was a happy place, after all. Now that I was happy there was nothing to fear.

I swung open the dungeon door.

A tentacle coiled around my waist. It yanked me into the air, shook me like a ragdoll, and laid me down on a floor made of bacon vultures. I was dizzy and nauseated. I puked up the utopian breakfast.

I looked up at the Cuddlywumpus. It was a giant shagpuff, hunched over and covered in furry tentacles. Each tentacle ended in an ear. Looking closely, I saw a mouth inside every ear and a hand inside every mouth. Its face was flat as a pancake's and blank except for two black button eyes. When the Cuddlywumpus cried out yesterday, it must have cried out from the mouths inside the ears on the tips of the tentacles. The Cuddlywumpus was hooked up to colorful machines. Pulsing green hoses ran from the Cuddlywumpus to the machines. They were either pumping something into the Cuddlywumpus or pumping something out.

The Cuddlywumpus mewed. It blinked its eyes at me as I approached the machines.

"Don't worry, I won't hurt you," I said. "I just want to know why Fanny keeps you locked away down here. You must be very important for her to keep you secret from everyone."

The Cuddlywumpus snuffled. It slapped its tentacles against the floor out of nervousness. To inspect the machines, I had to turn my back on the Cuddlywumpus. The beast appeared to be gentle enough. Timid, even.

The machines possessed no monitors, no gauges, no buttons or levers. I reached out to touch one and my hand passed right through. The machines were blocks of color. The machines possessed the physical immateriality of vapors exhaled from mouths on chilly evenings.

I reached for one of the ropes. Unlike the machines, the ropes were solid matter.

The Cuddlywumpus mewed again.

"Hold on, I only want to know whether something is going into you or out." I felt along the rope. "Hm . . . it's coming out of you." I looked at the Cuddlywumpus and scratched the top of my head. "What is coming out of you?"

The Cuddlywumpus averted its eyes.

I followed the algae-textured hose to the golden, immaterial machine connected up to it. I raised the hose to my mouth and chomped down.

I tasted maple syrup.

Maple syrup was being milked out of the Cuddlywumpus.

Where could all this maple syrup go?

The sea, I realized. Nowhere but the sea.

Something popped behind me. I spun around. The dungeon was filling with green balloons. They were identical to the balloons I'd seen Fanny release into the sky. The balloons floated through the dungeon darkness, vanishing. Wobbling, silent orbs. Like pickled spirits.

I circled the Cuddlywumpus to its backside and discovered that the balloons were emerging from the cuddlywumpus.

Above me, beyond vision, the balloons popped in a rat-tat sequence.

I remembered that Fanny Fod could come home at any time and I had no idea how long I'd been down there, so I patted a furry tentacle and left the dungeon, befuddled by my discovery.

I spaced out on the roof for the rest of the day. I looked up at some point and Fanny Fod was standing over me. Neither of us said anything. She wasn't really smiling, though she tried, and I knew I was trying, and failing, to smile as well.

"Did you have a good day?" I said.

"I've been home for a while," she said. "Have you enjoyed yourself?"

"Yes, thank you for breakfast this morning. It was the best breakfast I've ever had. I invented a shimmy in honor of it. Would you like to see?"

"The Cuddlywumpus is feeling unwell. I'm going down to the dungeon to stay with it awhile. I love the Cuddlywumpus so much. I can't stand to see it feel bad."

You don't love the Cuddlywumpus, I thought. Nobody would lock up something they love in a dungeon and then hook it to a bunch of machines to milk it of its goodness.

I retracted that thought. I couldn't think that way about Fanny. I knew she was only thinking of the greater good, if such a thing existed. I knew she was pure at heart and simply doing what she thought best, even if what was best to her seemed cruel and irrational.

"Would you like dinner in a while?" she said.

"Dinner would be fabulous."

A question formed on her peanut butter lips. She lowered her blueberry eyes. I sat up, my heart palpitating. My guts ached. Get it over with, I thought. Ask your question and crush me. You know I'm a bug. I'm not worthy of you, so end this quickly, gently. I will say I understand and politely return to my pickled plight.

"I'll be in the dungeon. Come inside in a while," she said. "Dinner will be waiting."

She left. I lay back and studied the green sky. I had done that. I was responsible for that. I had turned the sky green and killed a few pancakes, but even in my evil ways, I was better than these pancakes. I cared whether I was doing right or wrong. I deliberated every word and action. Happy pancakes cared as little about the moralistic value of their actions as sad pickles, perhaps even less.

Dinner was the same as the night before. It was only our second night together, but I got the impression that Fanny Fod could only make one thing. Granted, pancakes and maple beer were the best things ever. Even so, I wondered how long it would be before I tired of the monotony. The best things must get old at some point. I might even start craving brine chowder, for the sole sake of variation.

It was weird. We were totally meant for each other and we'd had such a great time last night, but neither of us seemed to feel much like being around each other right now. A nervous energy charged the air. It was apparent that we both had things to say to each other.

"You haven't touched your pancakes," I said.

"I feel full."

"How's the Cuddlywumpus?"

"You know that no one can ever find out about the Cuddlywumpus, right?" she said.

I shrugged innocently. "The cuddly what? You mean the Nothing in the dungeon?"

She smiled.

"I'm serious," she said.

"So how's the Cuddlywumpus?"

"Why are you so interested in the Cuddlywumpus?"

"Because I want to know this thing you love. I want to turn your love for the Cuddlywumpus inside out."

"I can't do this."

"Do what?"

"You were in the dungeon," she said. "While I was gone, you went down in the dungeon to see the Cuddlywumpus despite me specifically telling you not to do that. I told you that you were free to roam, but that if you cracked open the dungeon door even the slightest crack, you would not be welcome here. I threatened to kick you out. And you went and opened that door. You opened that door and you infected the Cuddlywumpus with your . . . well, you infected the Cuddlywumpus with yourself. So now I can't trust you in my castle."

I wanted to demand answers of my own. What was she doing keeping the poor thing locked up, milking it for all it was worth? Couldn't she at least provide the Cuddlywumpus a sunny room higher in the castle? But I was in no position to question her. She'd brought up her grievances first. Besides, this was her castle. Also, this was Pancake Island, not Pickled Planet. Arguing was probably taboo.

"Can you explain yourself?" she said.

I was festering. All my life, pickles had demanded explanations from me for the things I did. It was dangerous to try to explain what shouldn't be. It was better to be silent and let them think what they wanted.

"Well?" she said.

"Can we enjoy our dinner and talk afterward?" I said.

She lowered her head and picked up her glass and concerned herself with the beer. I took that as an affirmative. I had time to let my disjointed thoughts coagulate. Meanwhile, I turned my body over to my taste buds and gorged myself on pancakes and beer.

After dinner, Fanny and I went straight to bed. She did not check up on the Cuddlywumpus. She did not even speak its name. Fanny walked up the stairs in front of me, but I crawled into the big bed first. Like the night before, we gravitated toward the center. We wrapped our arms around each other. We wrapped our legs together. We could not have possibly been any closer. It was another greatest moment for me, but I felt that maybe it was not as great for her. Between the time I awoke and the time I noticed Fanny standing over me on the roof, something had changed. We were no longer the same pickle and pancake we had been the night before.

"I can't do this," she whispered.

She drifted off in my arms. No goodnight, no peanut butter kiss.

I fell into a dream about the faces. They tried to smother the zucchini castle. You will succeed, I said to them in the dream. You evil ones will succeed.

I did not want it to be true. I did not want the evil faces to succeed, because if they ever smothered me in my dreams, I would be lost forever. And now I had more than a dream to lose. I had Fanny Fod.

THE PICKLED APOCALYPSE

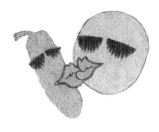

I awoke in shambles.

Fanny Fod writhed on the floor in a tangle of crepe blankets. Her blueberry eyes wobbled in their sockets. She was having a seizure.

"Fanny!" I said.

I took my skull in my hands. Shouting hurt my brain.

My right fingers met a wetness that was neither syrup nor brine. I jerked my hand away and looked at it. My hand was covered in green blood. Oh my, what had I done? I felt around my head and my fingertips fell into a hole clawed into the back of my skull. As I slept, I'd tried digging a hole to my brain. Why had I done this? What compelled me to tear away my own head? Now that I'd registered it, the wound hurt. Bad. The wound had not hurt before I noticed it.

I put my own pain aside and went to help her. Being soft and round and flat, her body absorbed most of the impact that could potentially result in severe brain trauma, a severed tongue, etc. I decided there was not much for me to do and waited for the fit to take its full course. I sat down beside her quaking body. How did I let this happen? I was unaware that epilepsy was contagious. I pinched myself so as not to retreat back into my own pain.

After a while, she scaled back down from the sulfuric

peaks of convulsion. She said that everything glowed.

"I want to be covered in light," she said. "I want to stand in the sun."

"Are you okay to walk? I'll carry you to the roof if you want."

"Don't worry about me. I feel spectacular. Yes, let's go to the rooftop." She looked at me, confused. "Your skull is bleeding. Why is your skull bleeding?"

"I woke up and found it that way. I don't know what happened. It's okay. My skull will feel better when we're in the light."

"Does it hurt?"

"It hurts."

"I'm sorry."

"It's okay."

Hand in hand, we went up the stairs to the roof to stand in the green light.

The air was damp and heavy.

We looked out at the world, and what we witnessed was all wrong.

Fanny let go of my hand.

Thousands of green pancakes swarmed across the island. They shuffled toward the zucchini castle, drooling and moaning.

"What's happened to them?" Fanny said.

"They've been pickled," I said.

I tried to take Fanny's hand, but she pulled away.

The pancakes surrounded the castle. Out in the distance, the sea shimmered. It was as green as the sun. Right beneath us, leading the pancake mob, the door-obsessed pancake stood beside the flattened, rocket-humping pancake boy. The two stared at me with sad, accusing facial expressions. The door-obsessed pancake raised her right hand and pointed at me. "You," she shouted. "You put me in this state." She was barely audible over the moaning crowd, but I heard her, and Fanny did as well.

"You've ruined happiness, Gaston Glew," Fanny said. "You've ruined happiness and you've lied to me."

She walked away. She left the roof. I made to follow her, but stopped short. There was nothing I could say or do. I'd pickled her planet and the last of her race. The prospect of a future together was bleak.

I stood on the ledge and peered down at the undead pancakes clawing and moaning at the zucchini door beneath. Fanny Fod was right. I had ruined happiness.

"Oh, Miss Door Lover, Mister Rocket Humper," I called. "I'm sorry for what I've done. I'm sorry. I truly am. Please accept my apology and turn back to your normal, happy selves. You're pancakes, remember? You can't remain dead forever."

But happiness was not eternal, or so the sun had said.

The dead green sun blaring down.

Every pancake in the front yard raised their flats heads to me at once. Their unmoving eyes fixed on me. Although green and sickly, the pancakes did not look depressed. They looked . . . hungry.

Pickle-shaped tongues lolled out of their mouths. The pancakes licked their lips and smacked their rotting gums. Together they moaned, "*Haaaaappppiiiinnnnesssss. . . .*"

That was when they tore down the door.

I ran to the stairwell and skipped down the steps. The Cuddlywumpus was in danger. I'd infected it, and in turn infected the syrup ocean, ruining everything, but Fanny Fod and I still might escape. With a lot of luck and a little leftover happiness, we could start a new colony somewhere else in the universe. If the last happy place was dead, we were its only shot at harvesting another.

I heard them shuffling around before I reached the

ground floor. I stumbled a few steps from the bottom and fell the rest of the way down. I sprang up, ready to defend myself against the pancakes, but they were not coming in my direction. Their pattering steps moved toward the kitchen. They'd broken down the front door in no time at all.

My arms trembled. They were almost too heavy to lift. I balled my hands into fists and tucked them beneath my chin. I felt so scared and alone, but if I didn't rescue Fanny and show these pancakes who was boss, the fright and aloneness would never go away.

I marched down the narrow hall that led from the stairwell to the kitchen. Three pancakes scuffled toward me. I swung my fists at them. Green syrup gushed from their bodies. I punched and punched, crushing them as if they were overgrown garlic spiders. But as soon as I'd mowed down the first batch, another came. Simultaneously, a chorus of moans broke out behind me. I flailed my arms, hoping to fight my way into the kitchen and to the dungeon door before the pancakes surrounded me in the hall.

I took down pancake after pancake. Their soggy carcasses piled up as they came into punching range. Soon, I wasn't just punching the brains out of the living pancakes, I was also kicking at the dead ones. I had to in order to keep moving forward. The moaning from behind approached fast.

I thought of the faces. The faces. The faces that would smother. I turned and ran back in the direction of the stairs, because in that moment, my fear of the smothering faces overcame my fear of losing Fanny, and by the time I overcame my own impulsive action, I was already running up the stairs. Pancakes swallowed everything beneath me.

The flapping sea of pancakes continued to rise. I had a clear path to the rooftop, but no way down from there. I'd have to face the smothering. I'd have to face it for real this time. I couldn't let Fanny Fod down anymore. After all that I'd taken, all I'd destroyed, to come all the way from Pickled Planet to find true love and manifest a nightmare, it had to come to this.

The words of the dead sun returned.

It is like being subject and object all at once. The boundaries between your perceptions and the world disintegrate.

That was the way it happened with Fanny and I during our first night together, when our lips met and we shared a yummy dream. We expanded beyond ourselves and swallowed each other. It was the greatest feeling ever.

I dove into the swarm of pickled pancakes. I resisted the initial urge to struggle, to swing my fists. Don't fight, I told myself. Don't fight don't fight don't fight.

I closed my eyes and let the pancakes drag me under. I envisioned their bodies as the molecules of Fanny's peanut butter lips, and that she was swallowing me whole. I sank deeper into the phosphorescent green confusion of bodies. A living lake of syrup and brine.

The pickled pancakes carried me toward the door of the dungeon. I could not see for myself, for the crowd blinded me, but they also propelled me forth. I trusted them now. They did not want to eat me or seek revenge for pickling their island. Maybe they were pickled, but so was I.

Sucking in mouthfuls of maple syrup and pickle brine, I thought how peculiar Fanny's and my children would taste, if we were to ever surface from this mess and she forgave me and we settled down and *WHAM!*

I slammed right into the dungeon door. The pancakes cleared a space around me, in which I staggered. No longer buried in pancakes, I was still up to my waist in fluids.

"*Haaaaappppiiiinnnesssss....*" the pancakes moaned.

I tried the door and found it locked. "Fanny, it's me," I called. "Everything is fine. We're safe. The pickled pancakes are our friends."

"Go away, Gaston. You're a disease," Fanny said.

"*Haaaaappppiiiinnnesssss. . . .*" the pancakes moaned, encroaching on the door.

"Everything is fine," I insisted. "How's the Cuddlywumpus?"

"Infected."

"I'm sorry."

"Just go away, and take the pancakes with you."

"Trust me, Fanny. I wouldn't lie to you."

"You already have."

"Well I'm not lying this time. I ruined happiness, I know. But listen, it's not as bad as you think. Trust me on this. I'm from the armpit of the universe. I know how bad things can be. Maybe these aren't the pancakes you're used to. Maybe they're not singing and dancing. Maybe they're less yummy than they used to be, but they're still pancakes. They just have a little of me in them, and don't you love me?"

"You remade my home, my life, everything I've ever known, in your own image."

"Isn't that what love's about?"

"You ruined everything."

"You keep saying that, but you're failing to see that it's not all bad. In fact, it may not be bad at all. These pancakes are spooky, but they're not evil. They're still your kin. Come on, give me a chance. Open the door. I want to see you. I want to hold you. Let me try to fix this."

"Go away, Gaston."

"I can fix the Cuddlywumpus."

The pancakes crowded close to me. I turned and batted them away. I gave them a look that said don't say a word.

I hoped their infected brains understood.

On the other side of the door, I heard Fanny speak to the Cuddlywumpus, and the Cuddlywumpus speaking back. At least the damned thing was alive. I pressed the right side of my head to the door. I resolved to be silent and wait for their talk to end.

Nothing doing.

The pancakes around me began to mutter.

"I feel so sad," said a pancake, muffled by the soggy crowd.

"I feel lonely," said another.

"I feel bad about the way I feel," a third said.

"Me too!" said the crowd.

I spun around and raised a finger to my lips. I shushed the pancakes. My hand shook and fell away from my lips when I saw what ailed them. They'd regressed further, into a pickled state so severe that the last of their happiness oozed from their porous flesh. Happiness turned to pus. Yellow and rancid.

"We're dying," they said.

"Be quiet. You're not dying," I said. I guessed the pickling had given them knowledge of a lot of grim stuff they'd been unaware of.

The kitchen and hall were clotted with their disintegrating bodies.

"Gaston, are you there?" Fanny said.

"Yes, I'm here."

"Thank you for your patience."

"Just open the door."

The pancakes were crying softly now.

"Open the door," I said.

The dungeon door swung open. I heard Fanny scuttle down the stairs. I stepped forward and stood on the top step. No glow emanated from the phantom machines. No ear-tipped tentacles writhed curlicues in the air.

"Fanny?" I said.

"Down here."

"Fanny?"

"Shut the door."

"I need a light."

"The Cuddlywumpus needs the dark."

"Can you turn on the syrup machines, just for a moment? When I'm down there, you can turn them off again."

"The machines are dead."

She wasn't going to reason with me. In the weak light coming through the crack of open doorway, I saw that the dungeon was filled with balloons.

The balloons obscured the hulking form of the Cuddlywumpus.

"Shut the door," Fanny said.

I gripped the railing in my left hand and turned to close the door with my right.

A pancake slipped in sideways before the door closed.

I stepped away from the door and tried to grab hold of the pancake before it scurried past, but the door swung open behind me. The door knocked me off balance. I teetered for a moment.

"*Haaaaappppiiiinnnessssss. . . .*" the pancakes moaned, as they surged into the dungeon.

I tumbled end over end.

Splayed out on the dungeon floor, I tried to stand, but the pancakes were coming down the stairs and they trampled me.

Fanny Fod screamed.

I threw wild punches. My fists tore through the groaning pancakes. Their syrupy guts piled up around me, forming a barricade that blocked the horde from trampling me any further.

I caught sight of Fanny. She stood beneath the Cuddlywumpus. The pancakes surrounded her on all sides. She spun circles, hitting the pancakes that came within range of her fists.

"Stay back!" she cried. "All of you, stay back."

"Fanny!"

She glanced at me as I struggled through the pancake guts and braced myself to break through into the circle of pancakes to help Fanny. But during her respite, the pancakes increased the pace of their onslaught by double. They shed their clumsy natures, moving now with a strength and agility they did not have before. They raised their heads, revealing rows of sharp, tiny, crystallized maple fangs, and they moaned, "*Haaaaappppiiiinnnnesssss. . . .*"

Before I could reach her, Fanny was buried in pancakes. I struggled forward, more desperate now than ever.

It did not appear that the pancakes took her down intentionally, but more like she had stood in the wrong place at the wrong time. They were piling up now, right where she'd stood. They crawled over each other, straining their newfound teeth and claws to get at the Cuddlywumpus, whose features now came into painful detail. The Cuddlywumpus had lost its fur. It was bald now, and green.

I knew I had infected the Cuddlywumpus. I could accept that. Harder to accept was the severity of the pickling. The Cuddlywumpus was in far worse condition than the pancakes.

Pickles sprouted from its flesh, obscuring its original form. The Cuddlywumpus looked like a seaweed-wrapped coral reef with a monstrous acne problem.

A gash split its belly in two. Green balloons floated from the wound. That was where the green balloons were coming from. The Cuddlywumpus was filled with green balloons.

The pancakes piled on top of each other. They struggled their way into the belly of the Cuddlywumpus, where they made attempts to eat the balloons, but the balloons popped beneath the pressure of their teeth and claws. They fell to eating the flesh of the Cuddlywumpus.

The Cuddlywumpus mewled and whined. The pickled pancakes, in conjunction with the chains holding it down, rendered the beast totally helpless.

I knew the only way to save Fanny was to rescue the Cuddlywumpus, but if the beast was going to make it out alive, I needed Fanny's help. There were simply too many pancakes in the dungeon.

I dove into the swarming mound.

I tore through soggy pancake flesh.

Pancakes bit into me, but they were only trying to get to the Cuddlywumpus.

As I searched for Fanny, I wondered about hump boy and the door-obsessed pancake. They had seemed intent on tracking me down when the pancakes first congregated outside the zucchini castle. The continuing pickled degradation must have torn apart their consciousness. They probably forgot all about me.

I called out to Fanny. She should've been screaming and she wasn't.

I clawed through pancakes faster and faster. I was almost buried in pancakes when I finally uncovered her.

The pancake pile had smothered her.

Fanny Fod was flattened, broken. I cradled her in my arms and brought my head to her chest. I detected a frail heartbeat.

I held her as close as possible without further ruining her body, warding off the pancakes swarming to eat the doomed and pickled Cuddlywumpus.

Pancakes crowded every available space in the dungeon. Syrup and brine sloshed up as high as my waist. Green balloons continued pouring forth from the gaping belly wound of the Cuddlywumpus. To reach the Cuddlywumpus now, the pancakes had to push through a balloon layer. The pancakes vanished as if the balloons were a low-hanging cloud strata. I heard them feasting. The Cuddlywumpus cried. At this point all I wanted was to carry Fanny Fod up the stairs, lock the dungeon door, leave the zucchini castle, and be rid of these pickled pancakes forever, but I feared that lifting her might kill her.

"Fanny, can you hear me? We must leave. We can't stay here. If you can hear me, I'm sorry about the Cuddlywumpus."

At the mention of the Cuddlywumpus, she twitched a little. Her bruised skin flickered a near-electric green before diminishing to a sick brown.

I thought she'd passed when a glimmer burst up in her eyes. "Gaston Glew, you've ruined happiness," she said. She was smiling.

I shook my head. "We can still be happy. We only need each other. The world never meant much to us anyway."

"Save the Cuddlywumpus," she said, her voice gargled and scratchy like a broken machine. "The Cuddlywumpus is the source of all happiness."

Her flesh glowed again. The name held a rejuvenating power over her. "My voice is decaying. My voice will be gone any moment. Whatever happens, know that I forgive you. I forgive you for ruining happiness. I forgive you for pickling my planet. I just hope that in your eternal plight, you find a way to forgive yourself for the terrible things you've done. I love you, Gaston Glew. May you always keep me alive in your heart."

"I love you, Fanny Fod."

I didn't understand. She looked as bright and beautiful as the day I'd met her.

And yet, she was growing.

As I held her in my arms, she swelled up like a balloon. The Cuddlywumpus, pancakes, and balloons already filled up the entire dungeon, and now Fanny Fod swelled, putting pressure on an over-pressured room.

When I could no longer hold her, I scrambled to my feet and tore through the pancakes separating me from the stairs. Climbing the stairs was like walking through a steep, thick wall of pancakes, but eventually I made it to the top. I turned around.

A pickled syrup sea was swelling in the dungeon.

Fanny Fod was almost as big as the Cuddlywumpus now. Each of her blueberry eyes was already larger than me. Whereas the pancakes smothered her before, now she smothered them. And green balloons clung to her body.

She kept expanding.

She grew as large as the Cuddlywumpus, and then larger.

She was an orb of pancake delight.

A macrocosm of her peanut butter lips opened up wide, giving the appearance that Fanny was splitting in half, and she swallowed the Cuddlywumpus.

An enormous tentacle-tongue curled out of her mouth. She licked her lips and the tongue furled back inside. Her peanut butter lips clamped into a smile. Somehow I knew they would never come apart again. Her mouth would never open up.

I tried to cry out to her in confusion, in mourning, but as my mouth opened and my cries pierced the air, she blew up. She exploded in gradient tremors of green and gold light.

Fanny Fod had achieved Yummy Decay.

PART Three

WINTERTIME

WELCOME TO THE WORLD OF FOD

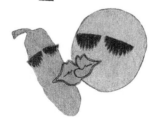

She birthed a new universe.

Her golden flesh stretched ever onward, forming the background fabric. The explosion diced her eyes into a billion shrapnel pieces. They shimmered in the fabric. The blueberry stars.

The remains of pickled pancakes floated on, collecting together into meteors and asteroids. Someday they would get very old and collide. Some of those collisions would form planets.

Everything smelled and tasted beery and syrup-sweet. The pickled essence trailed it all like comet tails, but the essence tainted nothing.

Beneath me or above me, depending on which way you considered things, Fanny Fod's peanut butter lips stretched for thousands of miles.

Her lips were a lonely island.

And on that island lay the Cuddlywumpus.

I traveled until I finally set my feet down on the surface of her lips. I stroked the hollow, half-eaten skull of the Cuddlywumpus.

I set to work burying all of its pickled tentacles in peanut butter so that someday it might take root and grow.

The Cuddlywumpus opened its eyes and blinked at me,

then its eyelids drooped and it fell into a deep slumber.

The Cuddlywumpus was beginning its new life as a tree. Someday it would blossom and grow edible fruit. For now it would sleep.

I had one last thing to do before parting from her lips.

I dug my hand into the peanut butter and carved a gigantic *U*.

I stood and stepped back to evaluate my work. I had intended to scrawl Captain Pickle's motto on the surface of her lips as a reminder to all future life, if there should be life, of the absolute necessity to march forth, to overcome the common struggle of all creatures no matter the cost. You did not have to be a pickle to understand what Captain Pickle meant when he said, "Unchain yourself from your briny fate, oh pickled prisoner!"

It struck me that when the Cuddlywumpus bloomed or life emerged elsewhere, fate would no longer haunt the creatures of the World of Fod, for with the creation of this world, fate dissolved. And that meant I was finally free.

I dug into her lips again and gave the *U* a tail, transforming it into a *Y* that stretched for miles. I worked for days without rest, trudging inch by inch to etch my new message into her peanut butter lips.

YOU ARE FREE.

My work here was finished. I had the rest of her body to sculpt.

In the wintertime of her universe, I floated on.

ABOUT THE AUTHOR

Cameron Pierce (b. 1988) lives in Portland, Oregon. He is the author of *Lost in Cat Brain Land, Ass Goblins of Auschwitz*, and *Shark Hunting in Paradise Garden*. His fiction and poetry has appeared in *Verbicide, The Pedestal Magazine, The Journal of Experimental Fiction, Bust Down the Door and Eat All the Chickens, Avant-Garde for the New Millennium, The Dream People, Bare Bone*, and many other publications. When he's not writing, he likes to ride bicycles and hang out at Lucky Lab, the greatest beer hall in the universe.

Bizarro books

CATALOG — SPRING 2010

Bizarro Books publishes under the following imprints:

www.rawdogscreamingpress.com

www.eraserheadpress.com

www.afterbirthbooks.com

www.swallowdownpress.com

For all your Bizarro needs visit:

WWW.BIZARROCENTRAL.COM

Introduce yourselves to the bizarro genre and all of its authors with the Bizarro Starter Kit series. Each volume features short novels and short stories by ten of the leading bizarro authors, designed to give you a perfect sampling of the genre for only $5 plus shipping.

**BB-0X1
"The Bizarro Starter Kit"
(Orange)**

Featuring D. Harlan Wilson, Carlton Mellick III, Jeremy Robert Johnson, Kevin L Donihe, Gina Ranalli, Andre Duza, Vincent W. Sakowski, Steve Beard, John Edward Lawson, and Bruce Taylor.

236 pages $5

**BB-0X2
"The Bizarro Starter Kit"
(Blue)**

Featuring Ray Fracalossy, Jeremy C. Shipp, Jordan Krall, Mykle Hansen, Andersen Prunty, Eckhard Gerdes, Bradley Sands, Steve Aylett, Christian TeBordo, and Tony Rauch.

244 pages $5

BB-001 **"The Kafka Effekt" D. Harlan Wilson** - A collection of forty-four irreal short stories loosely written in the vein of Franz Kafka, with more than a pinch of William S. Burroughs sprinkled on top. **211 pages $14**

BB-002 **"Satan Burger" Carlton Mellick III** - The cult novel that put Carlton Mellick III on the map ... Six punks get jobs at a fast food restaurant owned by the devil in a city violently overpopulated by surreal alien cultures. **236 pages $14**

BB-003 **"Some Things Are Better Left Unplugged" Vincent Sakwoski** - Join The Man and his Nemesis, the obese tabby, for a nightmare roller coaster ride into this postmodern fantasy. **152 pages $10**

BB-004 **"Shall We Gather At the Garden?" Kevin L Donihe** - Donihe's Debut novel. Midgets take over the world, The Church of Lionel Richie vs. The Church of the Byrds, plant porn and more! **244 pages $14**

BB-005 **"Razor Wire Pubic Hair" Carlton Mellick III** - A genderless humandildo is purchased by a razor dominatrix and brought into her nightmarish world of bizarre sex and mutilation. **176 pages $11**

BB-006 **"Stranger on the Loose" D. Harlan Wilson** - The fiction of Wilson's 2nd collection is planted in the soil of normalcy, but what grows out of that soil is a dark, witty, otherworldly jungle... **228 pages $14**

BB-007 **"The Baby Jesus Butt Plug" Carlton Mellick III** - Using clones of the Baby Jesus for anal sex will be the hip sex fetish of the future. **92 pages $10**

BB-008 **"Fishyfleshed" Carlton Mellick III** - The world of the past is an illogical flatland lacking in dimension and color, a sick-scape of crispy squid people wandering the desert for no apparent reason. **260 pages $14**

BB-009 **"Dead Bitch Army" Andre Duza** - Step into a world filled with racist teenagers, cannibals, 100 warped Uncle Sams, automobiles with razor-sharp teeth, living graffiti, and a pissed-off zombie bitch out for revenge. **344 pages $16**

BB-010 **"The Menstruating Mall" Carlton Mellick III** - "The Breakfast Club meets Chopping Mall as directed by David Lynch." - Brian Keene **212 pages $12**

BB-011 **"Angel Dust Apocalypse" Jeremy Robert Johnson** - Meth-heads, man-made monsters, and murderous Neo-Nazis. "Seriously amazing short stories..." - Chuck Palahniuk, author of Fight Club **184 pages $11**

BB-012 **"Ocean of Lard" Kevin L Donihe / Carlton Mellick III** - A parody of those old Choose Your Own Adventure kid's books about some very odd pirates sailing on a sea made of animal fat. **176 pages $12**

   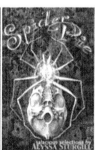

BB-013 **"Last Burn in Hell" John Edward Lawson** - From his lurid angst-affair with a lesbian music diva to his ascendance as unlikely pop icon the one constant for Kenrick Brimley, official state prison gigolo, is he's got no clue what he's doing. **172 pages $14**

BB-014 **"Tangerinephant" Kevin Dole 2** - TV-obsessed aliens have abducted Michael Tangerinephant in this bizarro combination of science fiction, satire, and surrealism. **164 pages $11**

BB-015 **"Foop!" Chris Genoa** - Strange happenings are going on at Dactyl, Inc, the world's first and only time travel tourism company.

"A surreal pie in the face!" - Christopher Moore **300 pages $14**

BB-016 **"Spider Pie" Alyssa Sturgill** - A one-way trip down a rabbit hole inhabited by sexual deviants and friendly monsters, fairytale beginnings and hideous endings. **104 pages $11**

BB-017 "The Unauthorized Woman" Efrem Emerson - Enter the world of the inner freak, a landscape populated by the pre-dead and morticioners, by cockroaches and 300-lb robots. **104 pages $11**

BB-018 "Fugue XXIX" Forrest Aguirre - Tales from the fringe of speculative literary fiction where innovative minds dream up the future's uncharted territories while mining forgotten treasures of the past. **220 pages $16**

BB-019 "Pocket Full of Loose Razorblades" John Edward Lawson - A collection of dark bizarro stories. From a giant rectum to a foot-fungus factory to a girl with a biforked tongue. **190 pages $13**

BB-020 "Punk Land" Carlton Mellick III - In the punk version of Heaven, the anarchist utopia is threatened by corporate fascism and only Goblin, Mortician's sperm, and a blue-mohawked female assassin named Shark Girl can stop them. **284 pages $15**

   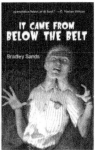

BB-021 "Pseudo-City" D. Harlan Wilson - Pseudo-City exposes what waits in the bathroom stall, under the manhole cover and in the corporate boardroom, all in a way that can only be described as mind-bogglingly irreal. **220 pages $16**

BB-022 "Kafka's Uncle and Other Strange Tales" Bruce Taylor - Anslenot and his giant tarantula (tormentor? fri-end?) wander a desecrated world in this novel and collection of stories from Mr. Magic Realism Himself. **348 pages $17**

BB-023 "Sex and Death In Television Town" Carlton Mellick III - In the old west, a gang of hermaphrodite gunslingers take refuge from a demon plague in Telos: a town where its citizens have televisions instead of heads. **184 pages $12**

BB-024 "It Came From Below The Belt" Bradley Sands - What can Grover Goldstein do when his severed, sentient penis forces him to return to high school and help it win the presidential election? **204 pages $13**

BB-025 "Sick: An Anthology of Illness" John Lawson, editor - These Sick stories are horrendous and hilarious dissections of creative minds on the scalpel's edge. **296 pages $16**

BB-026 "Tempting Disaster" John Lawson, editor - A shocking and alluring anthology from the fringe that examines our culture's obsession with taboos. **260 pages $16**

BB-027 "Siren Promised" Jeremy Robert Johnson & Alan M Clark - Nominated for the Bram Stoker Award. A potent mix of bad drugs, bad dreams, brutal bad guys, and surreal/incredible art by Alan M. Clark. **190 pages $13**

BB-028 "Chemical Gardens" Gina Ranalli - Ro and punk band Green is the Enemy find Kreepkins, a surfer-dude warlock, a vengeful demon, and a Metal Priestess in their way as they try to escape an underground nightmare. **188 pages $13**

BB-029 "Jesus Freaks" Andre Duza - For God so loved the world that he gave his only two begotten sons... and a few million zombies. **400 pages $16**

BB-030 "Grape City" Kevin L. Donihe - More Donihe-style comedic bizarro about a demon named Charles who is forced to work a minimum wage job on Earth after Hell goes out of business. **108 pages $10**

BB-031 "Sea of the Patchwork Cats" Carlton Mellick III - A quiet dreamlike tale set in the ashes of the human race. For Mellick enthusiasts who also adore The Twilight Zone. **112 pages $10**

BB-032 "Extinction Journals" Jeremy Robert Johnson - An uncanny voyage across a newly nuclear America where one man must confront the problems associated with loneliness, insane dieties, radiation, love, and an ever-evolving cockroach suit with a mind of its own. **104 pages $10**

  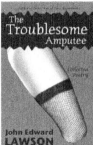 

BB-033 **"Meat Puppet Cabaret" Steve Beard** - At last! The secret connection between Jack the Ripper and Princess Diana's death revealed! **240 pages $16 / $30**

BB-034 **"The Greatest Fucking Moment in Sports" Kevin L. Donihe** - In the tradition of the surreal anti-sitcom Get A Life comes a tale of triumph and agape love from the master of comedic bizarro. **108 pages $10**

BB-035 **"The Troublesome Amputee" John Edward Lawson** - Disturbing verse from a man who truly believes nothing is sacred and intends to prove it. **104 pages $9**

BB-036 **"Deity" Vic Mudd** - God (who doesn't like to be called "God") comes down to a typical, suburban, Ohio family for a little vacation—but it doesn't turn out to be as relaxing as He had hoped it would be... **168 pages $12**

   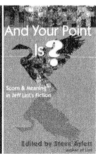

BB-037 **"The Haunted Vagina" Carlton Mellick III** - It's difficult to love a woman whose vagina is a gateway to the world of the dead. **132 pages $10**

BB-038 **"Tales from the Vinegar Wasteland" Ray Fracalossy** - Witness: a man is slowly losing his face, a neighbor who periodically screams out for no apparent reason, and a house with a room that doesn't actually exist. **240 pages $14**

BB-039 **"Suicide Girls in the Afterlife" Gina Ranalli** - After Pogue commits suicide, she unexpectedly finds herself an unwilling "guest" at a hotel in the Afterlife, where she meets a group of bizarre characters, including a goth Satan, a hippie Jesus, and an alien-human hybrid. **100 pages $9**

BB-040 **"And Your Point Is?" Steve Aylett** - In this follow-up to LINT multiple authors provide critical commentary and essays about Jeff Lint's mind-bending literature. **104 pages $11**

BB-041 **"Not Quite One of the Boys" Vincent Sakowski** - While drug-dealer Maxi drinks with Dante in purgatory, God and Satan play a little tri-level chess and do a little bargaining over his business partner, Vinnie, who is still left on earth. **220 pages $14**

BB-042 **"Teeth and Tongue Landscape" Carlton Mellick III** - On a planet made out of meat, a socially-obsessive monophobic man tries to find his place amongst the strange creatures and communities that he comes across. **110 pages $10**

BB-043 **"War Slut" Carlton Mellick III** - Part "1984," part "Waiting for Godot," and part action horror video game adaptation of John Carpenter's "The Thing." **116 pages $10**

BB-044 **"All Encompassing Trip" Nicole Del Sesto** - In a world where coffee is no longer available, the only television shows are reality TV re-runs, and the animals are talking back, Nikki, Amber and a singing Coyote in a do-rag are out to restore the light **308 pages $15**

BB-045 **"Dr. Identity" D. Harlan Wilson** - Follow the Dystopian Duo on a killing spree of epic proportions through the irreal postcapitalist city of Bliptown where time ticks sideways, artificial Bug-Eyed Monsters punish citizens for consumer-capitalist lethargy, and ultraviolence is as essential as a daily multivitamin. **208 pages $15**

BB-046 **"The Million-Year Centipede" Eckhard Gerdes** - Wakelin, frontman for 'The Hinge,' wrote a poem so prophetic that to ignore it dooms a person to drown in blood. **130 pages $12**

BB-047 **"Sausagey Santa" Carlton Mellick III** - A bizarro Christmas tale featuring Santa as a piratey mutant with a body made of sausages. 124 pages $10

BB-048 **"Misadventures in a Thumbnail Universe" Vincent Sakowski** - Dive deep into the surreal and satirical realms of neo-classical Blender Fiction, filled with television shoes and flesh-filled skies. **120 pages $10**

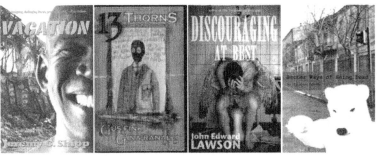

BB-049 "Vacation" Jeremy C. Shipp - Blueblood Bernard Johnson leaved his boring life behind to go on The Vacation, a year-long corporate sponsored odyssey. But instead of seeing the world, Bernard is captured by terrorists, becomes a key figure in secret drug wars, and, worse, doesn't once miss his secure American Dream. **160 pages $14**

BB-051 "13 Thorns" Gina Ranalli - Thirteen tales of twisted, bizarro horror. **240 pages $13**

BB-050 "Discouraging at Best" John Edward Lawson - A collection where the absurdity of the mundane expands exponentially creating a tidal wave that sweeps reason away. For those who enjoy satire, bizarro, or a good old-fashioned slap to the senses. **208 pages $15**

BB-052 "Better Ways of Being Dead" Christian TeBordo - In this class, the students have to keep one palm down on the table at all times, and listen to lectures about a panda who speaks Chinese. **216 pages $14**

BB-053 "Ballad of a Slow Poisoner" Andrew Goldfarb Millford Mutterwurst sat down on a Tuesday to take his afternoon tea, and made the unpleasant discovery that his elbows were becoming flatter. **128 pages $10**

BB-054 "Wall of Kiss" Gina Ranalli - A woman... A wall... Sometimes love blooms in the strangest of places. **108 pages $9**

BB-055 "HELP! A Bear is Eating Me" Mykle Hansen - The bizarro, heartwarming, magical tale of poor planning, hubris and severe blood loss... **150 pages $11**

BB-056 "Piecemeal June" Jordan Krall - A man falls in love with a living sex doll, but with love comes danger when her creator comes after her with crab-squid assassins. **90 pages $9**

BB-057 **"Laredo" Tony Rauch** - Dreamlike, surreal stories by Tony Rauch. **180 pages $12**

BB-058 **"The Overwhelming Urge" Andersen Prunty** - A collection of bizarro tales by Andersen Prunty. **150 pages $11**

BB-059 **"Adolf in Wonderland" Carlton Mellick III** - A dreamlike adventure that takes a young descendant of Adolf Hitler's design and sends him down the rabbit hole into a world of imperfection and disorder. **180 pages $11**

BB-060 **"Super Cell Anemia" Duncan B. Barlow** - "Unrelentingly bizarre and mysterious, unsettling in all the right ways..." - Brian Evenson. **180 pages $12**

BB-061 **"Ultra Fuckers" Carlton Mellick III** - Absurdist suburban horror about a couple who enter an upper middle class gated community but can't find their way out. **108 pages $9**

BB-062 **"House of Houses" Kevin L. Donihe** - An odd man wants to marry his house. Unfortunately, all of the houses in the world collapse at the same time in the Great House Holocaust. Now he must travel to House Heaven to find his departed fiancee. **172 pages $11**

BB-063 **"Necro Sex Machine" Andre Duza** - The Dead Bitch returns in this follow-up to the bizarro zombie epic Dead Bitch Army. **400 pages $16**

BB-064 **"Squid Pulp Blues" Jordan Krall** - In these three bizarro-noir novellas, the reader is thrown into a world of murderers, drugs made from squid parts, deformed gun-toting veterans, and a mischievous apocalyptic donkey. **204 pages $12**

BB-065 "**Jack and Mr. Grin**" **Andersen Prunty** - "When Mr. Grin calls you can hear a smile in his voice. Not a warm and friendly smile, but the kind that seizes your spine in fear. You don't need to pay your phone bill to hear it. That smile is in every line of Prunty's prose." - Tom Bradley. **208 pages $12**

BB-066 "**Cybernetrix**" **Carlton Mellick III** - What would you do if your normal everyday world was slowly mutating into the video game world from Tron? **212 pages $12**

BB-067 "**Lemur**" **Tom Bradley** - Spencer Sproul is a would-be serial-killing bus boy who can't manage to murder, injure, or even scare anybody. However, there are other ways to do damage to far more people and do it legally... **120 pages $12**

BB-068 "**Cocoon of Terror**" **Jason Earls** - Decapitated corpses...a sculpture of terror...Zelian's masterpiece, his Cocoon of Terror, will trigger a supernatural disaster for everyone on Earth. **196 pages $14**

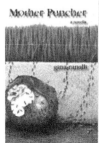 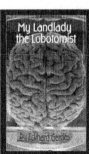  

BB-069 "**Mother Puncher**" **Gina Ranalli** - The world has become tragically over-populated and now the government strongly opposes procreation. Ed is employed by the government as a mother-puncher. He doesn't relish his job, but he knows it has to be done and he knows he's the best one to do it. **120 pages $9**

BB-070 "**My Landlady the Lobotomist**" **Eckhard Gerdes** - The brains of past tenants line the shelves of my boarding house, soaking in a mysterious elixir. One more slip-up and the landlady might just add my frontal lobe to her collection. **116 pages $12**

BB-071 "**CPR for Dummies**" **Mickey Z.** - This hilarious freakshow at the world's end is the fragmented, sobering debut novel by acclaimed nonfiction author Mickey Z. **216 pages $14**

BB-072 "**Zerostrata**" **Andersen Prunty** - Hansel Nothing lives in a tree house, suffers from memory loss, has a very eccentric family, and falls in love with a woman who runs naked through the woods every night. **144 pages $11**

BB-073 "**The Egg Man**" **Carlton Mellick III** - It is a world where humans reproduce like insects. Children are the property of corporations, and having an enormous ten-foot brain implanted into your skull is a grotesque sexual fetish. Mellick's industrial urban dystopia is one of his darkest and grittiest to date. **184 pages $11**

BB-074 "**Shark Hunting in Paradise Garden**" **Cameron Pierce** - A group of strange humanoid religious fanatics travel back in time to the Garden of Eden to discover it is invested with hundreds of giant flying maneating sharks. **150 pages $10**

BB-075 "**Apeshit**" **Carlton Mellick III** - Friday the 13th meets Visitor Q. Six hipster teens go to a cabin in the woods inhabited by a deformed killer. An incredibly fucked-up parody of B-horror movies with a bizarro slant. **192 pages $12**

BB-076 "**Rampaging Fuckers of Everything on the Crazy Shitting Planet of the Vomit At mosphere**" **Mykle Hansen** - 3 bizarro satires. Monster Cocks, Journey to the Center of Agnes Cuddlebottom, and Crazy Shitting Planet. **228 pages $12**

BB-077 "**The Kissing Bug**" **Daniel Scott Buck** - In the tradition of Roald Dahl, Tim Burton, and Edward Gorey, comes this bizarro anti-war children's story about a bohemian conenose kissing bug who falls in love with a human woman. **116 pages $10**

BB-078 "**MachoPoni**" **Lotus Rose** - It's My Little Pony... *Bizarro* style! A long time ago Poniworld was split in two. On one side of the Jagged Line is the Pastel Kingdom, a magical land of music, parties, and positivity. On the other side of the Jagged Line is Dark Kingdom inhabited by an army of undead ponies. **148 pages $11**

BB-079 "**The Faggiest Vampire**" **Carlton Mellick III** - A Roald Dahl-esque children's story about two faggy vampires who partake in a mustache competition to find out which one is truly the faggiest. **104 pages $10**

BB-080 "**Sky Tongues**" **Gina Ranalli** - The autobiography of Sky Tongues, the biracial hermaphrodite actress with tongues for fingers. Follow her strange life story as she rises from freak to fame. **204 pages $12**

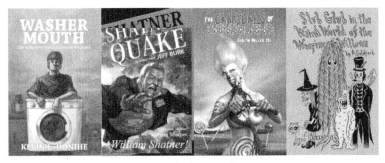

BB-081 "Washer Mouth" Kevin L. Donihe - A washing machine becomes human and pursues his dream of meeting his favorite soap opera star. **244 pages $11**

BB-082 "Shatnerquake" Jeff Burk - All of the characters ever played by William Shatner are suddenly sucked into our world. Their mission: hunt down and destroy the real William Shatner. **100 pages $10**

BB-083 "The Cannibals of Candyland" Carlton Mellick III - There exists a race of cannibals that are made of candy. They live in an underground world made out of candy. One man has dedicated his life to killing them all. **170 pages $11**

BB-084 "Slub Glub in the Weird World of the Weeping Willows" Andrew Goldfarb - The charming tale of a blue glob named Slub Glub who helps the weeping willows whose tears are flooding the earth. There are also hyenas, ghosts, and a voodoo priest **100 pages $10**

BB-085 "Super Fetus" Adam Pepper - Try to abort this fetus and he'll kick your ass! **104 pages $10**

BB-086 "Fistful of Feet" Jordan Krall - A bizarro tribute to spaghetti westerns, featuring Cthulhu-worshipping Indians, a woman with four feet, a crazed gunman who is obsessed with sucking on candy, Syphilis-ridden mutants, sexually transmitted tattoos, and a house devoted to the freakiest fetishes. **228 pages $12**

BB-087 "Ass Goblins of Auschwitz" Cameron Pierce - It's Monty Python meets Nazi exploitation in a surreal nightmare as can only be imagined by Bizarro author Cameron Pierce. **104 pages $10**

BB-088 "Silent Weapons for Quiet Wars" Cody Goodfellow - "This is high-end psychological surrealist horror meets bottom-feeding low-life crime in a techno-thrilling science fiction world full of Lovecraft and magic..." -John Skipp **212 pages $12**

BB-089 **"Warrior Wolf Women of the Wasteland" Carlton Mellick III**
Road Warrior Werewolves versus McDonaldland Mutants...post-apocalyptic fiction has never been quite like this. **316 pages $13**

BB-090 **"Cursed" Jeremy C Shipp** - The story of a group of characters who believe they are cursed and attempt to figure out who cursed them and why. A tale of stylish absurdism and suspenseful horror. **218 pages $15**

BB-091 **"Super Giant Monster Time" Jeff Burk** - A tribute to choose your own adventures and Godzilla movies. Will you escape the giant monsters that are rampaging the fuck out of your city and shit? Or will you join the mob of alien-controlled punk rockers causing chaos in the streets? What happens next depends on you. **188 pages $12**

BB-092 **"Perfect Union" Cody Goodfellow** - "Cronenberg's THE FLY on a grand scale: human/insect gene-spliced body horror, where the human hive politics are as shocking as the gore." -John Skipp. **272 pages $13**

BB-093 **"Sunset with a Beard" Carlton Mellick III** - 14 stories of surreal science fiction. **200 pages $12**

BB-094 **"My Fake War" Andersen Prunty** - The absurd tale of an unlikely soldier forced to fight a war that, quite possibly, does not exist. It's Rambo meets Waiting for Godot in this subversive satire of American values and the scope of the human imagination. **128 pages $11**

BB-095 **"Lost in Cat Brain Land" Cameron Pierce** - Sad stories from a surreal world. A fascist mustache, the ghost of Franz Kafka, a desert inside a dead cat. Primordial entities mourn the death of their child. The desperate serve tea to mysterious creatures. A hopeless romantic falls in love with a pterodactyl. And much more. **152 pages $11**

BB-096 **"The Kobold Wizard's Dildo of Enlightenment +2" Carlton Mellick III** - A Dungeons and Dragons parody about a group of people who learn they are only made up characters in an AD&D campaign and must find a way to resist their nerdy teenaged players and retarded dungeon master in order to survive. 232 **pages $12**

ORDER FORM

TITLES	QTY	PRICE	TOTAL

Please make checks and moneyorders payable to ROSE O'KEEFE / BIZARRO BOOKS in U.S. funds only. Please don't send bad checks! Allow 2-6 weeks for delivery. International orders may take longer. If you'd like to pay online via PAYPAL.COM, send payments to publisher@eraserheadpress.com.

SHIPPING: US ORDERS - $2 for the first book, $1 for each additional book. For priority shipping, add an additional $4. INT'L ORDERS - $5 for the first book, $3 for each additional book. Add an additional $5 per book for global priority shipping.

Send payment to:

BIZARRO BOOKS
C/O Rose O'Keefe
205 NE Bryant
Portland, OR 97211

Address

City   State   Zip

Email   Phone